I0663891

The 27 Club

Kevin Martin

The 27 Club
Copyright 2013 by Kevin Martin

ISBN – 1932809627
         978-1932809626

M-Press Publishing, Inc.
Las Vegas, NV

A Word from the Author

Since I have no idea where this new book may lead me, I am dedicating it to two other little mysteries in my life - as I write this my unborn (as of yet twins) Chase and Cassidy. We all can't wait to see you.

I also dedicate this with love to my wife Dawn, my children Brendan and Alyssa, and to mystery and conspiracy lovers everywhere – and you are everywhere, aren't you?

A book like this needs lots of editing and tender loving care and couldn't have been done without the help of another author in her own right; Judith Moose.

Thanks and love to one and all…

JULY 3, 1971

He woke up suddenly with a powerful urge to do only one thing… pee. He crept silently from his spot on the living room sofa to the bathroom in the hall of the tiny apartment, making his way gingerly in the dark using only the shaft of light cascading through the living room blinds from the street light outside to find his way. He didn't want to wake his new friend in the living room who he'd been partying with the night before. *That simply wouldn't be cool,* he thought to himself. He pissed for what seemed like an eternity, all the while wondering how much money on booze was flowing into the toilet water. He lowered the lid but didn't flush for fear of waking the others.

Stepping back into the hallway, he began to wonder what time it was. He knew it couldn't be dawn yet because he knew at dawn the city street lights would be off and they were still lit. Just as suddenly as the thought flashed across his mind the room around him was plunged into darkness when the street lamp, as if on his mental command, flickered off. He smiled at the irony and waited a moment for his eyes to adjust to the darkness to make his way back down the hallway to the living room when he heard a scraping sound at the front door to the apartment. It started slowly, tentatively. Then the light from the interior stairs spilled inside the living room as the front door was slowly opened.

A burglar, he thought at once. Slowly, he crept a few paces backwards until he was standing in the bedroom just past the bathroom. He crept behind the half-open bedroom door and began to think about whether or not he might find something, anything, a weapon preferably, to defend himself with.

He could see the intruder was wearing a white jacket of some kind and carrying something in his right hand. *Why would a burglar be in white and not black*, he thought.

The intruder crept out into the living room, closing the door behind him without making a sound, once again plunging the room into darkness. The intruder was in the living room where his new friend lay asleep. He heard some small sounds, nothing too terrifying or ominous. It sounded like the intruder was fumbling in a briefcase or a bag of some sort. Perhaps he found something to steal and was putting it away. But what? He didn't remember anything of value in the living room worth stealing. Surely he was looking for jewelry or something of value.

My God, he thought. *Was he taking jewelry off his friend while he lay passed out on the sofa? Could he still be out cold from the debauchery of hours ago? Why hasn't he awakened and seen the intruder for himself?*

He hated not being able to see anything. Maybe he should make a noise to try and spook the intruder. He thought better of that plan, not knowing if he had a weapon himself and whether or not his friend would be the one to catch the brunt of his plan.

A few minutes later the intruder crept back to the center of the room in line with the hallway in front of him, his silhouette a little clearer in the doorway set off by a crack of light around the door from the hallway lighting outside. He now stood not ten feet from him when the intruder suddenly switched on a flashlight, shining it down the hallway right at him. The beam struck on the opened door frame only inches from his face, and spilled into the bedroom he was hiding in.

Every thought came to him in a jumble, every plan of action. *If he cried out to alert the others they would awaken not knowing the score and he would only endanger them. What if the intruder had a weapon? Surely he did.* He sat instead in silence, stunned and paralyzed in fear.

Then, as quickly and quietly as the intruder appeared, he was gone. He switched off the flashlight as he swung open the front door, briefly emitting light into the apartment. He could see the intruder was a man in dark pants and a white top like a doctor would wear, and carrying a black bag by its short handle like a doctor would carry. But he knew this was no doctor. He knew the intentions were sinister. He felt it while he watched it all unfold.

Once the door clicked shut, he crept into the living room to the door and quietly as he could, twisted the lock. *Hadn't it been locked before?* he thought. Unsure, he went to the blinds and peered carefully out one bent blade to the deserted street below, watching and waiting to see if the intruder crossed his field of vision. In a minute, the figure appeared, but without the street lamps on and only the night sky for illumination, he couldn't see his features well enough to learn any more about his identity. The intruder darted across the street and down an alleyway. No car. He must have had friends waiting.

Feeling a bit safer now, he switched on the living room overhead light and began yelling out to his friends. "We've been robbed!" he yelled. "Wake up! Wake up! There was a burglar just now. Didn't you hear anything?"

The girl on the chair stirred first. She had been lying passed out in the chair and had slid to the floor, her mini-skirt now around her waist with no panties on.

I'd normally dig this scene, he thought if he hadn't just been scared to death.

"Are you okay?" he asked as she came around.

"Yes, why wouldn't I be?" she asked, wiping the sleep from her eyes. "What's going on, are you tripping?"

"No I am not tripping. A burglar was just here."

"Here? In here?" she said gesturing in the air with one hand. "Maybe you were dreamin' man."

"Yes in here, and no, I wasn't dreaming. I was in the loo peeing and…"

"What happened then?" she asked, now fully awake.

"I don't know."

"Who was it man?"

"I don't know. I told you. He came in while I was in the loo and crept around you guys. I stayed in the bedroom looking for something to defend myself with, a baseball bat or something like that. I don't know if he had a weapon and I couldn't very well jump in not knowing, you know? We could've all been killed if it was some burglar spaced out on drugs looking for some money or something to sell. He wasn't here long and he left."

He looked to the sofa. "Wake him up!" he shouted to her about his friend.

She shook the man slumped on the sofa. "Wake up honey..."

He didn't stir.

"Pam, wake him up. We have to call the police," he said again with a stronger tone.

"I'm trying to," she said. "Help me wake him."

He shook him and said, "Wake up, dude!"

"Oh shit!" she exclaimed.

"What?" he asked turning away and picking up the telephone.

"Oh shit man, I don't feel a pulse," she said, pressing her fingers into the man's wrist. She put her head on his chest and then drew up in fright, the blood rushing from her face and she grew visibly paler. "Oh my God... I think he's dead!"

"Dead? What!" he exclaimed while putting the phone back down.

"Yes, dead."

"I'll call an ambulance," he said. He picked the phone back up and dialed for the operator. "Operator, yes, I need an ambulance fast to High Street."

As he hung up the phone he asked the girl, "What time is it?"

She looked at her watch and answered, "4:15. Why?"

"Just wondering," he said.

By 5:15 the people of the world would hear the news for themselves... Singer Jim Morrison was dead.

CHAPTER ONE

42 years have passed since the horrible day the world discovered Jim Morrison was dead. In a high-profile auction house in California, John Black and Stanley Simpson sit waiting for the chance to purchase a piece of the past.

"Tell me again WHY you are going to bid on these Jim Morrison letters?" Stanley asks impatiently.

"He was an important part of Rock 'N Roll's early development," John answers.

"As was Vanilla Ice," Stanley sarcastically notes.

"I said important, early, and development Stanley. Maybe I should have added influential."

"Influential? What's more influential than 'Ice, Ice, Baby…Ice, Ice, Baby? What a hook!"

"Do you really want me to answer your questions, or are you just screwing with me again?" John asks, noticeably perturbed.

"No, I really want to know. I'll be good. I promise," he says, holding up the Boy Scout three-finger promise in the air.

"Uh huh…" John says, in a disbelieving tone. "This group of letters is rare because firstly, he didn't write many at all, making all of his autographed material rare and valuable."

"I don't write letters so my handwriting must also be rare and valuable, huh John?" Stanley interrupts.

"People have to want to buy your autograph Stanley."

"Okay, point taken. Go on…"

"Secondly," John continues, "These particular letters were written from Paris and sent by him to Los Angeles. This was while he was in Paris looking for his muse just months before he overdosed and died."

"So did the muse kill him John?" Stanley says sarcastically.

"Cute."

"Muse?"

"Yes muse. You do know what a muse is, don't you?"

"Yes. I believe that's the Greek for heroin right?"

"You really don't care about this so why are you asking me questions?"

"No, I care. Don't be so touchy John… I am trying to show some interest, but it's just that some letters home to the old ball and chain or whoever he was writing to still seems awfully boring and unimportant to me, and I just want to know why you thought this would be a good buy for us."

"He had an interesting writing style, and he himself often said he was more of a poet than a songwriter. He even published books of poetry."

"So these are interesting letters full of poetry?"

"Yes. I mean no… I mean, from as much information as they have released, they seem interesting, but not full of poetry."

"Let me see your catalog," Stanley says, reaching for the book. "I want to read about them again."

"The letters are not printed in the catalog, jackass."

"You're interested in buying letters, you have no idea what they say, and I'm the jackass in all of this?"

"Okay, I'm sorry." John says in a retreating tone.

"Better."

"It's just that I know you're not really interested so I'm wasting my time trying to explain it all to you."

"You know the agreement between us John. You're the brains, and I'm the money and connections. Besides, I was just busting your chops. If you say we're going to make money on this deal, then let's pick us up some Jim Morrison letters and then go get some dinner."

Stanley was in investment banking. More specifically, he was in the estate division of a large bank; the kind that kept gobbling up smaller banks in their race to be the largest or only bank left. When an estate that had items to liquidate in its inventory, items that were antique or collectible in nature, Stanley would call John, who was an expert in such things, and they would try and profit off of their expertise. They had made quite a lot of money this way in the past. Usually John would evaluate the item for the bank's liquidation team, but in so doing was often allowed first crack at buying some of the items outright before auction.

This event between the two became known among them as "having a death in the family," a funny kind of code phrase Stanley dreamt up years before and would use when calling John on an estate deal that sounded promising.

This was different though. It was one of those times when John had found the lead on something he thought his experience could help him buy and the two would make their money when he resold it.

In the case of the Morrison letters, John had what he called a "fish on the line," meaning a buyer with deep pockets who wanted the items but didn't know how to obtain them himself. Often the very rich are so busy getting and maintaining their money, they don't have time to pursue things they called the way, say, a school teacher collecting beanie babies would go out on the weekend to scour garage sales for more of her stuffed treasures.

In the case of the very rich, it takes most of their time just being rich, so when something catches their eye, as these letters had for John's client, John would be paid well by simply buying them and then quoting a higher price to the client – a mark up for his time and expertise. He also guaranteed to the client that the items in question were worth the price, and were, most importantly, authentic to begin with. A lot of forgeries exist in the autograph market, and a lot of inexperienced people deal in the market even at the very top of the ladder and sell questionable material to unsuspecting collectors.

In fact, only a few years before one of the largest autograph dealers in the country had been in the middle of one of the largest sales of forged items, peddling Marilyn Monroe and John F. Kennedy contracts that supported the long-held belief that Marilyn had a relationship with the slain president. It turned out neither had signed the contracts, and John, who had a chance to look at some of them along with another legend in the field who has since passed away, knew they were not authentic, but that didn't stop the dealer from selling a few million dollars worth of them to collectors until they were proven to be forged.

So in the case of rare collectibles like these Morrison letters they would eventually, if held long enough, catch up to the value the fish or the client paid, which would be high, but how does one set a price on a one-of-a-kind item that more than one person would like to own? It's really an inexact science when it comes to pricing it and ultimately ends up being worth what someone is willing to pay for it. John had the "someone" on the line, and now he needed the letters at a good enough price to mark up for a profit for Stanley and him to split.

John wouldn't out and out gouge someone on price. He still had principles, and believed you could shear a sheep more than once but only kill it once, so he preferred leaving the client feeling good so he could sell more to them at a later date.

Stanley, on the other hand, had no such qualms about positively ripping someone off on something, but John was in this and so many other ways, the yin to his yang, and they had always been a good balance for one another ever since they became friends in high school.

Stanley went on to a banking career and a financial double major, while John majored in this and that, changing majors constantly, playing professional student while learning and pursuing his real love of all things historical and collectible. Once their individual careers began to mesh in this pursuit, they both made very good money at it, and John and Stanley had sold one item or another to nearly every museum, major collector, and Hollywood celebrity in the past 20 years of doing this together.

So here they were on a bright, sunny California day, sitting on folding chairs in a drab, cement walled building, about to bid on the letters in an auction of rare autographs. Stanley hadn't eaten since his plane landed, making him especially cranky and John hadn't wanted Stanley to come at all, but Stanley refused to back the deal financially without seeing what John was all fired up to buy.

"Okay I'll bite," Stanley said. "Why aren't the contents of the letters printed in the catalog John?"

"Because they have never been printed is exactly the point. They are what you call unpublished, and the buyer today gets the publishing rights when they buy them."

"So they can sell forty-year-old news to the Enquirer of something like that?"

"Yes, despite your obvious sarcasm, you're not actually that far off."

"So did he say anything interesting in the parts you were allowed to read? Something worth publishing?"

"They only allowed you to read small excerpts and then they gave a basic description of the overall content in a general way. That part is on page 32. Here, read it for yourself," John said, pushing the open catalog onto Stanley's lap.

"Okay... Lot 139, Jim Morrison archive," he read aloud. Still not completely getting it, Stanley looks at John and says, "Ooh, it's an archive John. That sounds really important to me already."

"Archive only means an assemblage of more than one letter or document. Now shut up..."

"Morrison writes back home to Ma," Stanley continues.

Thoroughly annoyed, John tosses a look towards Stanley. "It doesn't say that; so if you're going to editorialize or paraphrase then read silently to yourself!"

"Alright John. Stop being so touchy. Letters include," he continued reading out loud, "stating he was depressed. Hmmm...depressed followed by an overdose. John, this sounds fishy to me." Stanley looked while saying that with a mocking grin.

"I'm going to say crap like that at your funeral too Stanley."

"What makes you think you'll outlive me John? Haven't you ever heard the expression 'only the good die young?'?"

"Comments like that one for example..."

"Reading on," Stanley said. "Hey John, there are only a few lots away. Better get out the 'Ole Master Card. OH MY GOD!!!"

"What's wrong?" John asked, nearly jumping out of his chair from the shock of Stanley screaming.

"The estimate for these letters is 10-15 thousand dollars! Is that a typo? Please tell me that's a typo John!"

"No, it's not a typo. You screamed at me for that?"

"You could buy a new car for that kind of green John! Are you smoking something?"

"What new car is $10,000 to $15,000 these days? And no, I am not smoking anything Stanley."

"I saw one of those nifty Prowler cars up the street when we were coming in and the front windshield said "Loaded – Only $16,000 John."

"I think I'll stick to my Mercedes if that's okay with you."

"A very iconoclast remark there Johnny. Not exactly keeping with the spirit of Morrison, would you say? I mean, can you see Jim tooling around in a 500SL Mercedes John?"

"Shhh... It's SL 500, not 500 SL, and if I miss this lot coming up I will bury you in that Prowler."

"They do look an awful lot like a hearse, don't you think? Or some Nazi German old-timey car?"

"You ever see a hearse painted metallic purple?"

Smiling smugly, Stanley said, "You DID see it when we came in! John, I knew you did."

"I saw it, now hush." John quickly glared at Stanley, "I mean it."

"Okay, okay… Reading on… It says he mentions 'The Doors'."

"His group," John said

"I am your age John. I know it was his group."

"I was just beginning to wonder if you had any idea of the importance of these letters, that's all."

Stanley continues reading. "And it says he was leaving the group. Well, well, he never really knew how prophetic that statement was, did he?" He laughs at what he thinks is a joke.

"You understand you're making fun of the dead right?" John asked.

"I've had a few years to get over his passing. John lighten up." Returning his attention to the catalog, "Oh, ooh, ohh," Stanley grunted.

"What are you, a child? You sound like that guy on 'Welcome Back, Kotter'."

"You mean Arnold Horschack?"

"I guess. Jesus! How do you remember the character's name?"

"Because he was a road map of exactly what you didn't want to act like in school if you held out any hope at all of ever seeing a girl's who ha up close. A mission that became almost quest-like for me."

"Yeah, you're a regular 'Sir Lancelot'."

"You know John, not everyone is cut out to be a monk."

"I'm not a monk."

"No, but you are clearly one of those guys who seems content with having only seen pussy close up once when you were born."

"If I miss this lot coming up because of your inane prattling on and on, I swear to God I will…"

Stanley gets the message and interrupts him. "It also says he mentions a stalker in the letters. I don't think these letters are authentic John."

"And why is that Einstein?" John is obviously still losing patience with Stanley's line of questioning.

"It says stalker John. Like I said that's not a term we used in 1969 or whenever he died."

"First, he died in 1971, and more importantly, it you'd pay attention when you're reading, the word stalker is in quotes in the catalog, meaning they were paraphrasing and not using his exact words."

"Oops! You are correct about that one John, I'll give you that. I was only doing my job as the investment banker here and trying to protect our imminent investment Johnny. Just channeling a little 'Milburn Drysdale' to keep the 'ole money in the account you know." Lightly amused, Stanley adds, "Now Drysdale, he was a classic performer."

"*Beverly Hillbillies*, right?" asked John.

"Right. John I am so proud of you for knowing that."

"Yes, it was a cute and funny show. I saw it growing up."

"But you wouldn't shell out ten grand for a stack of 'Milburn's' letters right?"

"If Raymond Bailey, who was the actor who played 'Mr. Drysdale' on the show had the same affect on actors and acting as Jim Morrison had on popular music, then yes I would."

"Ooh, ooh," Stanley says looking down at the catalog in his lap.

"Now what are you reading?"

"It says here he mentions Jimi and Janis in the letters. I expect that means Hendrix and Joplin."

"Yes, I read that part too."

"Now that part does sound cool. Do you think they were friends or was he being bitchy in the letters?"

"Being bitchy?"

"Yeah, like 'you know," Stanley says, changing to an awful Southern accent, "that Jimi can sure tear up a guitar, but Janis is nothing more than a hillbilly from Texas who likes to drink and...'"

"What is God's name makes you think Morrison had this awful Southern accent you're doing?"

"Sorry. I was probably still caught up in my *Beverly Hillbillies* recollections."

"Yes, you must have been. Now shut the fuck up. The lot is coming up next I think..." John takes the catalog back from him.

CHAPTER TWO

The lot was shown on a small television screen next to another screen that showed the current bid in several different monetary systems simultaneously, such as the Euro, Japanese Yen, the French Franc, and U.S. Dollar. The bidding opened with the amount of bids that had been previously left by other bidders, known as absentee bidders, and started at the estimated price of ten thousand dollars. Before the bidding was released to the room of dealers and collectors around John and Stanley, more bidding began, this time from a bank of telephone operators to the right of the auction podium, who were all on the phone with bidders from all over the world.

The lot certainly proved interesting to more bidders than just Stanley and John, and although John held his bidder number aloft for a few minutes, his bids weren't even taken as the bids between. The phone lines ran up the price quickly on their own.

Dejected, John finally put his hand down as the lot neared twenty thousand dollars and before he could even discuss the option of bidding a little higher with Stanley and safely selling the lot to his client at a higher price, the lot continued to soar past 30, 40, and finally just over $55,000, not even counting the buyers premium, which is the percentage the auction house charges the winning bidder on the lot they won.

In this case it was 20%, meaning the winning bidder would have to pay $55,000 plus a buyer's premium of another $11,000, for a total of $66,000. Over six times what the auction house had estimated the lot to sell for.

"Wow! Did we get outbid or what John?" Stanley asked, almost in a daze.

"I don't know how. They really can't be worth this price," an utterly dumbfounded John replies.

Stanley shrugs his shoulders and stands up. "Oh well, off to another deal. Any leads while we are still in town?"

John shakes his head emphatically, "No, we are not off to another deal. This shouldn't have happened."

"Really John, I know you're competitive and all, but..."

"No, it's not that. Twice, or even a few times the estimate maybe, but I'm sure this was a world record."

"So it's a world record. So what? They do happen at auctions you know. We've seen them before."

"Not like this... Not buying a pig in a poke so to speak. Remember they supposedly didn't allow anyone to read the letters, and had the content been worthy of 60 plus thousand, they would have had to leak some of the contents to the collectors to achieve that kind of price."

"Again I say so. What are you thinking happened here then?"

"I think the winning bidder and maybe even an under bidder may have known more of the contents than the other bidders like us. That's what I think Stanley."

"Well you know as well as I do that they don't need an under bidder to run up a bidder if the bidder left a high maximum they were willing to pay or foolishly told the auction house that they would pay whatever to obtain them," Stanley looks inquisitively at John. "You think the auction house cheated and gave someone the letters previously to read in their entirety? Is that what you're saying to me?"

"Maybe… And in the last $30,000 in bids, they had two phone bidders, so they would have had to do it at least twice to bid off of each other and drive up the price."

"Not necessarily," Stanley points out. "The second line could have been bullshit like I said, or are you just mad that you weren't considered a serious enough bidder to be "in the loop" so to speak? This goes back to high school John. You were never really one of the cool kids and I know it pisses you off whenever…"

He's cut off by an irritated John. "Look Sigmund Freud, I don't have to be one of the "cool kids" to know when I'm being cheated!"

"Cheated how," Stanley asks. "You mean a fake bidder to run up the other guy?"

"They wouldn't be the first auction house guilty of shill bidding."

"John, you of all people know that's against the law." Stanley proclaims.

"Stanley, so is the speed at which I operate my vehicle most of the time, but in the words of the late, great, Richard Nixon, it's only against the law if they catch you."

"I know you don't want to get thrown out of another auction house because you couldn't keep your comments to yourself, or do I need to remind you of last year's little incident?"

"That auction house was selling forgeries and you know it."

"Yes, I believe you, but you aren't allowed to bid there anymore are you? That is the bottom line John. Try and focus here. If we don't learn from our past we are destined to repeat it. Isn't that what you're always telling me?"

"Yes, but it's cheating and unfair," John says in an exasperatingly raised voice.

"So is cheating on your taxes but a lot of people do it John."

"More importantly though is why would any bidder pay such a ridiculous price for essentially what is sight unseen material?" John reiterated.

"Okay, I agree you may be on to something John, but there is nothing we can do now. Spilled milk and all that..."

Looking to the podium, John remarks, "On the screen it says the winning bidder prefers to remain anonymous. Why the winning bidder was anonymous also bothers me."

"How do you know they want to be anonymous?"

"Read the screen on the final tally. It says phone bidder anonymous."

"Oh, okay. I'll give you that one, but come on John. You yourself know sometimes bidders are anonymous for a variety of reasons. Tax dodging, etc… Some people don't want to resell the item and they know people like you, as an under bidder, would contact them, which would be a major pain in the ass."

"Maybe…"

"Sure, sure."

"But if we could find out the consignor's name and meet with them, I'd feel better."

"Feel better?" Stanley asked with feigned disbelief.

"Yes."

"How about a drink and we call it a day instead? I'm not Dr. Phil you know."

"No."

"Okay, how about a massage at the Oriental 'Spa'," he said with air quotation marks.

"No," John said, more testily.

"Okay. Okay. It was probably just some big autograph dealer John."

"Maybe, but I've never heard of these letters being on the market before now."

"Well then maybe some member of the Morrison family needed some dough and broke them out."

"There are no heirs still alive Stanley." John disapprovingly shakes his head. "I don't know, Stanley. Something's not right in all of this."

"There are too many variables for you to be getting your nose out of shape like this John. Come on. Really now."

"Look Stanley - autograph dealers for the last three decades would have pestered the hell out of any heirs to sell anything related to Morrison like these letters."

"Ok. So let's look at this hopefully one last time, okay John?" Stanley asks before continuing. "Jim writes someone back in Los Angeles, that we know, right?"

"Yes."

"And he wrote while he was touring in Paris, right?"

"Yes, he had left The Doors and was going to Paris to write some new poetry, relax, and decide his next direction."

"Okay… He link up with anyone there?"

"Yes. Pamela Courson, his girlfriend."

"Okay, so he wasn't writing her?"

"No. The catalog says the letters were to his mother."

"Okay. You said the auction house also stated the letters were postmarked to Los Angeles, right John?"

"Right. But I'm not sure if he went and she followed or what," John said. "Look Stanley, history records he went to Paris, got an apartment with Pamela, and died there of an overdose in his bathtub."

"No tours?"

"No tours."

"No impromptu jam sessions?"

"No."

"But the letters were sent to Los Angeles, not Paris?"

"That's what the catalog states."

"Maybe the catalog was wrong. Maybe the USPS postmarked them in Los Angeles, but not Paris when they arrived." Stanley suggests.

John looks at Stanley like he has a screw loose. "The USPS has nothing to do with it. There was a Paris postmark, and more importantly, the catalog says they were addressed to his mother in Los Angeles."

"I hate the post office." Stanley remarks.

"What?"

"They are always so damn smug when I go in there."

"Maybe it's your attitude to them." John suggests.

"Don't be such a boy scout John. They don't go in to work packing heat and blowing each other away because they like their jobs you know."

Trying to get back on track, John starts analyzing again. "If he was writing to Pamela, he wouldn't have sent them to her previous Los Angeles address if he knew she was already in Paris. Besides like I said, the catalog states they were to his mother."

"I know, but that sounds less promising or exciting doesn't it John? I just thought maybe the letters were for Pam but sent in care of Mom. Had you thought of that?"

"Maybe, but I don't think so. I'd need to do some research on when Pamela came to Paris to be sure."

"I'm just trying to justify the content and price they fetched." Stanley says.

"They sold much higher than they should have," John says. "Period."

"In your opinion."

"Yes, in my expert opinion, remember?" John corrects him.

"Okay, okay. Calm down. I wasn't trying to challenge you. I know you usually bat a thousand on these kinds of things John, but let it go. Don't make this about ego."

"Stanley, there was no mention of an unpublished poem or song."

"So you told me before. So what?"

"That would have made them much more valuable. So why did they sell so high?"

"How the hell should I know? You're the expert, you tell me!"

"Unless..."

"Unless what?"

"The only explanation is that someone knew the content already."

"We keep circling that tree John, but we'll never know for sure. You can't just go up to the auction house president and say, 'Excuse me, but did you leak the contents of these letters to drum up some good business and the shill bid bloke up to his limit, screwing us out of a deal' and he'll say, 'Oh, yes. You got me. Where are the cuffs? I knew it couldn't last.'
You're not 'Columbo' you know. Although you look like you are following his bathing and clothing habits." Stanley says while giving John's appearance a once-over.

"I woke up late and didn't have a chance to take a shower."

"Okay, but John, if someone knew the complete content… You said that was the value in the letters; the content right?"

"True."

"So why pay through the nose if they'd gotten a peek at them? If they knew the content, they could sell the content without owning the letters right?"

"Maybe they didn't want anyone else to read them."

"Why would that be John?" Stanley asks.

"Maybe Morrison talking about the stalker was something the buyer didn't want anyone to know about."

"I see. So now you are saying a stalker 40 years later pays a king's ransom to keep some letters mentioning that Morrison believed he had a stalker from coming to light and identifying him or her?"

"A stretch I know, but what if…"

"A stretch John? Look, I know you're always 'Mr. Optimist' but that's a stretch like putting Pavarotti in spandex! John it's just not right. You're embarrassing yourself at this point, stop it."

"Why couldn't that be true?"

"Because it's a billion to one shot that's why, and we have already determined you are NOT 'Lt. Columbo' nor are you that lucky."

"But what if that were the truth?"

"Oh God," Stanley moans. "Okay, let me humor you for a minute here John. Where do you want to go from here on all this superstition and supposition pray tell?"

"We need to find the buyer or the consignor."

"Information they aren't likely to give us."

"True." John concedes.

Adjusting his clothing, Stanley offers John an alternative. "Look. Let me talk to the little damsel in charge of that computer over there," he says while gesturing to a girl behind a desk and computer across the lobby from them, "and see if she can help." Raising his eyebrows in a coy manner, Stanley continues, "I'll lay out some Stanley charm for you free of charge if it means we can get on with our lives."

"It does."

"Okay, fine." Stanley makes a final clothing adjustment.

John, putting a damper on Stanley's macho man moment tells him, "She already knows we want the information, by the way."

"What!" Stanley looks at John almost stunned. "How's that?"

"Before you got here I asked her for that same information."

"Why would you do such a thing?"

"Because she looked like a minimum wage flunky and I thought she might give me some information we could use if the auction wasn't won by us, which it wasn't. There is an advantage to knowing who you are bidding against. You know that!"

"All the more reason to let ME handle this then..." Stanley says as he runs his fingers through his hair.

"Okay, sure, knock yourself out," John says, gesturing towards the woman.

"Do you doubt my masculine persuasions John?"

"She's not going to give up information like that. I told you she wouldn't tell me, and they'd probably fire her for giving out personal information on bidders or consignors at any rate. What are you going to do differently than me, ask her out?" John laughs at his joke.

"Whatever it takes my unbelieving friend, whatever it takes. The key to that sentence was that she wouldn't help YOU."

"Did you notice if she was even single Stanley, or gay? I'd hate for you to blow all that mojo of yours in vain," John says smirking.

"Look John, you blew your end of this surefire money making deal, as I remember you called it that on the phone, so let 'Uncle Stanley' bail your ass out okay?" He adjusts his clothes and turns back to John. "A little faith in my legendary skills with the ladies if you don't mind."

"Okay, knock yourself out, Stanley. Really, KNOCK yourself out!" John says, shaking his head as he watches Stanley saunter across the floor of the auction house.

CHAPTER THREE

Stanley struts over to the reception area where a pretty young girl of around 25 sits typing in front of a computer screen.

John had always hated the charm Stanley seemed to so easily display with the opposite sex and had to always try to be content with the fact that the ladies in their lives usually started off being attracted to Stanley, but then ended up with John. He secretly hoped that the fact bothered Stanley as much as Stanley's getting them at the start bothered John. He knew deep down it probably didn't because Stanley lost interest in a girl fairly quickly, always seeming to enjoy the chase more than the capture.

John was a serial monogamist, always going relationship to relationship looking for his soul mate. Stanley didn't believe there was such a thing. *Looks may have something to do with it after all,* he thought. Stanley was tall and had a great head of hair that pissed John off every time he caught Stanley running his hands through it, whereas John's hair was thinning. Hell, it was thin at birth and never was that thick. In addition, by his late 20s, he was relegated to wearing glasses. He had tried contacts but his eyes were just too dry to keep them in, so he had to wear glasses for distance. Stanley always made fun of his vanity in taking them off every time he was indoors or had the chance to.

Women, of course, always said glasses didn't matter to them, but John would always say that no one could name a Hollywood celebrity considered to be hot by the public at large that wore glasses. Neither could Stanley.

Why is it, he thought, *that sunglasses are so damn cool even indoors but eyeglasses aren't? Was it just the tint that changed everything?*

At any rate, John rationalized their inequality with the opposite sex away by reminding himself daily that Stanley was all in all about as deep as a cupcake, and not even as filling! Personality is a great equalizer for looks, although having money helps you no matter what the hell you look like. Another sore subject between the two of them...

Stanley was so anal about spending money, outside of on women that is, that you couldn't pull a needle out of his ass with a tractor. John, on the other hand, held the Biblical view on money and of the ant saving up for the coming winter: practical and safe, but his Achilles heel was always the collectibles he dealt in. He was a geek at heart and loved holding historical items in his hands and would forgo eating if it meant he could acquire, even briefly, something significant. The items he coveted didn't warrant honorable mention in Stanley's book though. In fact, John could only ever interest him in an item by reminding him what they might get for it should they sell it. Then the banker side of Stanley would come to the forefront.

Leaning on the counter on one arm, he lowers his gaze to hers just as she looks up to see if she can help him. He speaks first, cutting her off. "My, my, no one's eyes are that naturally beautiful. So tell me, where did you find that shade of contact lens?"

"I'm not wearing contacts," she said back to him.

"No, really, come on… It's just you and me here. No one else is around. I won't tell your secret," he said, putting his fingers to his lips as if to hush himself.

"I'm telling you the truth," she says.

"My friend over there," he said, gesturing at John sitting in the waiting area. "He can't hear us. Come on, come clean. It's just that the color, I've never seen it before. It's really breathtaking. Worth every penny you spent."

"I swear, they are one hundred percent me," she says, giggling a bit this time and subconsciously widening her eyes open further.

"Wow," he says. "You're telling me the truth then?"

"Yes," she says even more proudly than ever.

"Liz Taylor has nothing on you girl!"

"Oh, stop now…" she says.

"No, no, really, I mean it. She has those legendary violet eyes, but yours are really special."

Leaning in closer to the girl, she responds by leaning forward, almost tipping out of her chair, nearly face to face when Stanley whispers, "They're chemically altered you know…"

"Liz Taylor's?"

He nods, "Yep."

"Really?"

"I know someone who knows someone. Shhh…" he says, placing his fingertip to his lips again and looks around.

"You can do that?" she asks in astonishment.

"Honey, if you have enough money, you can do anything you'd like to yourself. You'd be surprised. I'm Stanley, by the way, Stanley James."

"Hello," she says, extending her hand and shaking his demurely. "My name is Barbara, Barbara Bain, and yes, I know everyone tells me there was an actress by that name."

"Yes, she played on the original TV series 'Mission Impossible'. Well, that makes you a 'Mission Impossible' girl too, I suppose. What a pity," he says with a sly smile."

"Not necessarily," she says, biting her lower lip just a bit.

"Oh good, I like a challenge, but not something that's impossible," he says, smiling suavely while she giggles. "This isn't your only job, is it?"

"Well, yes it is. I'm full time here. Why do you say that?"

Still laying on the charm, "I mean you must also model right? I understand if you don't want to tell me, stalkers, and all of that, but…"

"Oh no, I have never modeled. My mother always told me I was too short to model."

"She was probably just jealous of you. What a shame…My mother always told me dynamite comes in small packages."

She smiles and stifles a small giggle this time.

I think I'm going to be sick, thinks John as he intently listens from a few feet away. He gets up and walks closer to them, pretending to admire different items in a snack machine, when he really just wants to listen closer. *I should leave his ass here, but I have to know if she knows anything. It just galls me that he's already made more headway with her than I did. What is it about him?*

"You must enjoy the atmosphere around here."

"It's always different, that's for sure," she acknowledges.

"It must be exciting when prices go high on things."

"Yes, I can't believe what some people are willing to pay for stuff I wouldn't pay a penny for, you know?"

"Yes I do." Moving in for the kill, Stanley mentions, "My friend and I were here to bid on those smelly old Jim Morrison letters. My friend digs him." Lowering his voice, Stanley continues, "He's older than me, and I thought we had certainly brought enough cash to seal the deal, you know, and then suddenly, WOOSH!" he said loudly with his hand thrown out like an airplane taking off, making the receptionist jump in her chair. "Off the prices went, you know?"

Bastard, John thought. *We are one year apart you vain bastard.*

"Yes, I was watching when it happened. I couldn't believe that one either."

"That's why I thought it would be cool to find out who the consignor was, cause I thought maybe, just maybe, he had other letters and could sell us more at a more reasonable price, you know?"

"Can't blame your train of thought there, but I can't help you because they'd fire me for giving out consignor's information."

"Oh, too bad, but I understand."

Good girl, John thinks smugly.

"At least the dealer who sold them must be pleased with the price they got, huh?" Stanley asks, starting his own fishing expedition.

"Normally you'd be right. We do have a lot of regular dealers who consign things to us, but not in this case."

"Not a dealer?"

"No. It was a private consignment from a woman, but like I said before, I can't tell you her name."

"I understand," Stanley says. "But how do you know she isn't a dealer?"

"It's a real nice, elderly woman who I think could really use the money. She isn't a dealer. Trust me on that."

"Those always seem to be the ones that win big, don't they?"

"How do you mean?" she asks.

"I mean like Power Ball or the lottery."

"The lottery?"

"Sure, whenever it goes off in the millions and millions, it always seems to be some elderly person who wins. Have you ever noticed that? Never some 20-year-old like you."

"Oh, I'm not 20," she says blushing, "but I do know what you mean."

"This lady must have been a big Morrison fan too, huh?"

"Oh, I don't think so. She didn't seem to know much about him actually. When my boss spoke with her, I was there for the meeting taking notes for him. She said she didn't know what all the fuss was about."

"Didn't you think to ask if she knew him? Morrison, I mean. That would be cool to talk to someone who actually knew him."

"You really are a big Morrison fan too, like your friend, aren't you?"

"Well, a little. Like I said, he seems to make my friend over there happy." Stanley says, still trying to schmooze his way to an answer. "You aren't a Morrison fan though, huh? Too young, I understand. It's okay."

"No, I like some of his songs, but like I said, I can't really say much more, but I did think to ask her something like that when we spoke once later. She said she had never met him, and she wasn't a relative of his or anyone else in the family."

"No? Fascinating…"

"Nope." She leans in towards Stanley. "Listen, you're cute, but my boss would be angry if he knew I gave out any information about her. Worse still, they'd fire me or sue me."

"Sue you?"

"Sure," she says. "They tell us all when we're hired. They've done it in the past. We all sign confidentiality agreements that say they have the right to sue us for giving up proprietary information things we learn here on the job. You don't want my unusual eyes all unemployed now, do you?" she says, batting her eyelashes at Stanley in a cute manner.

"No, no… I don't want your husband mad at me either," he says smiling.

"No husband here," she said, holding out a bare left hand with no rings.

"Really?" he asks like a spider to a fly.

"Nope. Are you married?"

"Oh no, but I'd love to someday."

"But," she added for him.

"Well," Stanley hesitates, "I'm just too sensitive, too romantic."

"Oh, I don't think there's anything wrong with that. Maybe you've just been with all the wrong women," she says coyly.

"Maybe… Hey, you know what? There's a new restaurant in town called Mickalis. Would you like to have dinner with me there tonight?"

"The Mickalis?! My God, my own boss couldn't get in there when he tried! There's a waiting list. Very snooty I'm told. You can really get us in?"

"Absolutely."

Looking over at John, she asks, "What about your friend over there?"

Yeah, what about me? John thinks as she mentions it.

"Oh, he has other plans."

That son of a bitch! John thinks, still listening in.

"Well I'd love to go. Just the two of us. Thank you!"

"Not at all…" he says smiling broadly. "When do you get off tonight?"

"Six o'clock," she replies.

"Six is perfect." How about I pick you up at 6:15?"

"Oh," she says, putting her hand on her head. "I look dreadful. I would need to go home and change."

"You don't look dreadful from where I'm standing." Stanley adds, "I won't have time to change either, so fair is fair, yes? We'll bum in there together and show them snooty folks what's what."

"Okay, I guess. I'm so excited. They say celebrities eat there all the time. No telling who we might see!"

"Okay, it's a date then?"

"See you at 6:15," she says.

Walking back over to John, Stanley slumps into the chair next to him and in a low voice says, "Did you hear all of that?"

"I didn't catch the consignor's name if that's what you mean." John says sarcastically.

"Patience, John. I'll get it from her at dinner tonight."

"You think so, huh?"

"Well sometime tonight anyway, if you get my drift," he says, winking at John.

Unenthused, John replies, "I get your drift. How are you getting into this Mickalis place anyway?"

"I have no idea," Stanley says. "That's your end of this deal."

"Are you nuts?" John asks angrily.

"You've always been good at crashing places John. You have that aura of respectability about you. Besides, did you really expect me to do it all for you, do you? Call in some favors John, if you want me to go there with her."

"Couldn't you have met at McDonald's instead?"

"She wouldn't get loose enough to tell us what we want to know at the golden arches, John. Don't be so cheap."

"Hamburger Hamlet then. The food's good there."

"Yes, and everyone who lives here has been there a hundred times. Besides, not special enough. Nobody spills their guts at a placed called Hamburger Hamlet, John. Get real…"

Knowing the score, John says, "You just want to romance her on my dime."

Nodding his head in agreement, Stanley adds, "Think of it as a fringe benefit. I was the one who wanted to go on to that other auction in New York City, remember? I can't take too much time off from the bank you know, but you insisted on pissing away our time on a deal that you queered…"

"I did not queer the deal. I just didn't count on the price increase."

"Look John-John. I'm just trying to help you get your little closure so we can move on with our lives and make money on some other new deal."

"It's hardly taking one for the team though is it? She's gorgeous."

"Don't be a hater John. It's not a pretty side to your personality."

"What if she still doesn't tell you the consignor after all this?"

"Always doing a worse case scenario on things aren't you John? My plan is to tell her that we're not collectors, but really journalists."

"Journalists?"

"Yes, working on a story about Morrison as journalists. Surely she's heard that we, as journalists, will go to jail rather than to reveal our sources. In other words, her sources. You savvy? Real Bernstein and Woodward kind of shit. Very Deep Throat, get it? Get it John?"

"I get it Stanley. You're going to take this hot girl out and try a plan you call 'deep throat.' That much I believe."

"John, you make it sound tawdry... So dirty..."

"Just as long at the end of it all you get the consignor's identity for us."

"For you, John." Stanley says, driving the point home. "Not for us. There is no way to make money on this deal anymore. It's dead to me and should be to you, but for whatever reason, it's not. So I'm just being a pal here and trying to help you gain some peace of mind, and after I'm done helping you out, I am on the next plane back home. You dig?"

"No, it really is for us." John indicates.

"Really? How so?"

"Maybe it's true, what you said back there. What if the consignor does have more letters and we can buy some for our client?"

"After the record price he had to pay, why would he sell us any at any reasonable rate?"

"You know many times you and I have been after one thing, only to find a better, bigger deal on something else."

"Okay, okay. I'll give you that. We have nothing to lose. Any more I mean. So I'll get the consignor info from Barbara there, and we'll go see the consignor, but if there's no profit to be hand then color me gone. I'm not getting all obsessed like in some conspiracy theory John. Agreed? Now let's split this place," Stanley says.

"Agreed," John says, as they both rise to walk out of the auction house.

"Let's move hotels to something nicer, since this is looking more like a vacation anyway." Stanley says as they walk into the underground parking garage, handing the lot attendant their ticket.

"Where do you suggest Mr. Moneybags?" John asks.

"A nice suite. Maybe at the Beverly Hilton."

"I am not going to agree to spend money like crazy to get you laid."

"I can get laid any time I want, and even at a Motel 6, but do you want us to look like respectable journalists or not?"

"Respectable journalists can still stay at the Holiday Inn."

"Marriott, it's my final offer."

"Okay, deal. But not a suite."

CHAPTER FOUR

They drive just a few miles to a Marriott they'd stayed at in the past near Universal City, where a lot of the tourists stay when visiting Hollywood. They pull into the valet service area and get a strange look, as they only have two toiletry bags they want sent to their rooms. After all, they hadn't thought they'd be staying so they didn't pack anything.

"Great. He thinks we're a couple Stanley."

"So." Stanley says poking fun. "What, you could do better?"

"Cute."

"Couple or not John, I am not sharing a room with you!"

"Why not?"

"Why not? You are so cheap John. Because I may bring that little senorita back here for some more intensive interrogation and I don't need you dampening the mood."

"I don't even know what that means, but okay. I'll agree to separate rooms, but no room charges on my card. You never pay me back. Okay? The restaurant bill is likely to be high already. No booze by the way, please."

"You could ruin a wet dream, you know that John?"

John nods at an irritated Stanley, "I need to call a few friends to get your damn reservation, so if you will excuse me."

"Then what are you going to do?"

"What do you care?"

"Aw, your ass is really burning over this girl, isn't it?"

"NO!"

"You're cute when you pout. Let's please remember you drug me into this and wanted this information."

"Okay, okay, but spare me the salacious details."

"Big word, salacious. Who talks like that?"

"Anyone educated. It means…"

"I know what it means, but that doesn't mean I have to use it in everyday conversation John."

"Now who's the hater Stanley?"

"I am not a hater of your vocabulary. I'm merely trying to say you may alienate a few young hotties talking like a professor."

"I have a degree and could have been a professor, so should I instead sound like a gangster? Would that be better for you?" John asks in a huff.

"The expression these days is gangsta John, and no, you don't have to sound like a gangsta, but somewhere in between might raise the success rate of your pursuits John. Really, I'm only trying to help."

They check into separate, but adjoining rooms. Stanley leaves to go pick up his new date while John thumbs through his infamous black book to find a name of someone who could get him the reservation at Mickalis. *Why must that son of a bitch make everything so hard on me*, he thought as he dialed the phone.

"Danny?" John asks when the other end is answered. "It's John. I need a favor man. I need to get two into Mickalis for dinner tonight. Can you help me?"

"John," the voice on the other end answers, "You at Mickalis? Are you popping the question to some young lovely?"

"No, no. It's not for me."

"Owe someone big huh? That place is a fortress ever since it became a hot spot for Paris Hilton and her crowd."

"You know I don't give a damn about celebrity watching. I just need this for a business deal."

"It's not going to be pretty man."

"How much?"

"I gotta hit the Maitre 'D hard. This is Friday night John and I don't know who all is going to be there."

"Well I need the reservation for 7:00. Doesn't that help?'

"Yeah, yeah, for sure. No one legit wants to be seen there before 9:00, 10:00 tops."

"What's it going to cost me?"

"300."

"Dollars?"

"No pennies, yes dollars! Come on John, you know better."

"Okay, okay. I've just had a rough day. Put it in the name Stanley James plus one."

"Is the 'plus one' hot?"

"She's cute."

"Then why aren't you the one plussing her?"

"Danny, I'm tired and I just want to watch a movie and take a shower. I'll explain sometime when I see you. Now don't forget me."

"I won't. I'll do it right now."

"You're the best."

"I know. Ciao!"

Hanging up the phone, John jumps into the shower, all the time muttering under his breath about Stanley's choice of restaurant.

Danny was incredibly well connected. He had been paparazzi back when they still called themselves photographers and before they were the favorite target of hatred around tinsel town. He branched out into a kind of concierge status, scalping tickets, reserving seats for the power brokers in Hollywood. They'd known each other for years and years after running into one another at an auction once and had been friends ever since, but friends who did business together. Danny had a heart of gold but put the J in Jewish. When it came to money, it was always business is business. Still, all in all, you could usually count on him and he was glad he didn't have to dig further to get Stanley and his plus one into the trendy Mickalis, on the same evening he called no less!

After getting out of the shower, John waits for Stanley to return. He turns on his laptop and surfs the web for more on Jim Morrison's tumultuous life.

A few hours later, Stanley returns and before he even has a chance to knock on John's door, John swings it open and walks into Stanley's room.

Stanley looks at the open door. "Knocking is foreign to you, isn't it John?" he asks while getting up to close the door. "I might have had my date up here you know."

"I doubt that. Besides, I heard you coming down the hall, looked out my door first, and saw you were alone. Well?"

"Well what, John?"

"Did you get any information from her?"

"Naturally…" Stanley says smugly.

"Of course. How insolent of me to ask." John replies. "So… Who is the consignor?"

"Some old lady named Birch."

"Birch… Was she related to Morrison?"

"Nope… She says the old lady was friends with Morrison's mother and got the letters from her before she died."

"Okay. Anything else?"

"No, not much."

"An address?"

"She drew the line there, but I got something just as good."

"How's that?"

"The old lady is coming in tomorrow to be paid."

"Tomorrow? Too soon, no way."

Stanley continues, "Babs said she worked out an early payment with the auction house."

"Did she say why they agreed to that?"

"Yes. Said the Birch broad needs the money to move into a retirement home with helpers. Nursing staff and stuff, and the auction house agreed to pay her but only because the buyer paid so quickly."

"And they knew that would happen how exactly?"

"Okay. Okay, so they knew they had a fish by the tail."

"Yeah, and I just wonder what line they fed the fish to get them to pay early, and to pay so much. The sale was today Stanley."

"Yep, I know. I was there, remember?"

"And he had thirty day terms to pay," John continues. "Everyone gets that long but…"

"But," Stanley interrupts, "your mystery guy, he paid shortly after the auction ended, and they already gave him the letters. I know all of this because I was working to get my little liebchen to make us a copy on the sly."

"She would've done that?" John asks incredulously.

"No, probably not, but, I was trying that angle anyway when she told me they already gave the letters to the buyer, actually his representative to be exact."

"And the buyer's identity?" John asks hopefully.

"Sorry, no trifecta here…"

"Why not?"

"She truly doesn't know, on account of the way they protect buyers who wish anonymity. They assign them a number only to identify them by, which they did of course with your guy. And his number, not that it will help you any, but FYI, it's 1625. I wrote it down on this napkin after she told me. She wasn't happy about giving me the info and thought I was writing it down."

"Which you were."

"Yes I was, but I faked her out by saying I was actually writing down what she was wearing on our first date, to always remember her by on my little napkin. A little love souvenir."

"Which she bought?"

"Of course."

"Naturally…"

"Uh, huh. Anything else?"

"No John. I think I have done enough work for you. Why can't we leave this alone? It's not going to go anywhere."

"How do you know that?" John asks.

"I don't I guess, but come on John. The odds are long on this one and besides, I was thinking…"

"Oh God, no, not that!" John jokes.

"Yes, I was, and I was thinking even if you are right and something fishy is associated with this sale, it's only going to piss someone, or someones, off that we are looking into it. Someone with enough extra cash lying around to sink over sixty thou into Jim Morrison letters plus buyer's premium I might add."

"And how do you figure that Stan?"

"Barbara said the buyer was almost paranoid in how he handled the auction house."

"How does she know?"

"Her boss told her he was extremely specific in that no one sees all of the letters."

"Did she or her boss say why?"

"Yes, same thing you said before, that the value lay in them being unpublished."

"Yes, but you see why that doesn't work for me?"

"No, I actually don't."

"Follow me. If you were going to publish them anyway, your identity should not be any big deal. In fact, you would want people to know you set a record buying them and were set to publish them."

"Why?" Stanley asks.

"Because, very often, when that happens other similar items are flushed out of collections and the sellers contact you first knowing you ponied up so large for the other pieces. It's a win-win and you can always refuse any offers that come your way.
I would understand for tax reasons anonymity, but the sum isn't in the millions like some paintings. Same for anonymity because of fear of theft. These are one-of-a-kind letters and imminently traceable and too hard to sell or fence, and again, not enough money for all that trouble."

"And publishing makes money on sales?"

"A book, movie, anything, and anything being sold to the public benefits from publicity, so you would actually more likely hold a press conference announcing your find and what you intend to do with it."

"Whet the appetite of the public for the upcoming missive or film?" Stanley asks.

"Exactly," John says.

"Okay, I see your point but still, does that make it so clandestine?"

"No, maybe not, but it does make it odd and interesting." Changing subjects, John asks, "Was she nice?"

"Was who nice?" Stanley asks innocently.

"The girl! The girl you got the information from!"

"Jealous?"

"No… I mean, a little, probably. She was cute."

"And a great kisser…"

"Oh God. Enough!"

"But you asked me…"

"I only asked you if she was nice, not if you kissed her."

"She was nice."

"Thank you for your help."

"Reeeeeal nice." Stanley makes a point of holding out the real.

"Okay, thanks, I got it."

"Very accommodating in every way," Stanley continues unprompted.

"I get it. Now drop it. You're just being mean now."

"Okay, okay. I didn't sleep with her okay?"

"Really?" John says with a look of disbelief.

"Really," Stanley says.

"You're just saying that."

"No, I swear. You were camped out in my room. Where would we have gone idiot?"

"What do you know? A woman who could resist your charms."

"I didn't say that. Don't jump to conclusions John. I said I didn't sleep with her."

"Well what else? Could it be you're embarrassed to admit that you struck out for once and didn't get to sleep with a girl on the first date?"

"No, I'm not. You said you didn't want any details and I'm trying to respect your wishes."

"I don't believe that, but I'm very happy to hear the truth."

"Yes, it's true. I didn't sleep with her."

"Well there is a God. She looked like a sweet, wholesome type to me when I saw her."

"Don't judge a book by its cover. Those are always the wildest, John."

"Not this time Tiger."

"Well, actually…" Stanley's words trail off.

"Actually, what? You didn't sleep with her. You said so yourself!"

"Yes, that's true, but…"

"But what? I was right in the middle of my assessment of her. Class act that girl."

"Period." Stanley adds.

"That's right, period. End of subject. You finally struck out."

"No, PERIOD. As in 'Aunt Flow' is what I meant."

"What?"

"She was on her period, so we rescheduled the sex for Sunday night."

"What?" John asks, his voice getting even higher and sounding more desperate.

"You pushed it John. I was going to leave it alone, but you pushed it."

"Are you going to see her Sunday night?"

"Are we going to still be here in town Sunday night John?" Stanley asks.

"NO!"

"Where will be then, pray tell?"

"I don't know, but not here."

"Are you punishing me John? For helping no less?"

"No, I just doubt very much that we'll still be here, that's all."

"Okay John, whatever you say." Stanley says with a smile.

"Stop smirking at me. It has nothing to do with your little rendezvous with the whore."

"The whore? Okay I see, a minute ago she was marrying material and now she's a whore."

"Well isn't it obvious?"

"Because she found me attractive, that makes her a whore?"

"No, because she wanted to bone you on the first date and then rescheduled. THAT makes her a whore!"

"If you were going to bone me, as you put it, it would make her a man, not a whore."

"You know what I mean."

"Yes, I'm afraid I do. Hater."

"Just drop it okay?"

"Okay, okay," Stanley says but then continues. "Have you ever noticed the way those little applicator cases tampons come in look like spent rifle cartridges? I think the designer was trying to warn us John. What do you think?"

"I think I don't think about bizarre shit the way you do. That's what I think."

"Are you a tampon man, or a maxi-pad man John?"

"I try not to have to use either actually. What kind of stupid question is that!?"

"I'm sorry. Sometimes I forget that you haven't had as much "experience" with the ladies as I have," Stanley says, putting air quotation marks around the word experience.

"If by "experience" you mean "social diseases" then yes, you are correct." John mocks Stanley with the same quotation mark signs with his fingers.

"That's just something people who don't get laid like to say. Though isn't it like people who go on TV all the time and say 'I love the way I am. I wouldn't want to be skinny. Those fat fucks lie, and so do you!"

"I party as much as the next guy."

"Really? Doing what?"

"I have hobbies, things I like to do. Intellectual things that you wouldn't understand."

"My grade point average wasn't that far off of yours, Mr. SAT score."

"No, but you took simpler courses."

"I'm waiting. What do you do to unwind then?"

"I told you I have hobbies."

"I'm listening…"

"I like magic tricks. You know that."

"Magic tricks? You're making this too easy on me John. You're just supporting my hypothesis about your loser status with the broads."

"Loser status? I'll have you know magicians are the new rock stars."

"Who told you that? A magician I'll bet. John, David Blaine and his crowd like Chris Angel wouldn't get laid on a bet if they weren't famous with money. THAT is the real magic with women, trust me, or do you really think a hot girl wants to tell her girlfriends she's dating a magician?" Stanley keeps going, despite John's thoroughly annoyed demeanor. "Don't answer that. Listen John, unless in your fictional, dysfunctional hypothesis she is porking someone like David Copperfield or Chris Angel, your theory doesn't hold up the idea that magic is partying, or rock star status, or something a hot chick would be attracted to."

John interrupts. "You forgot to mention Siegfried and Roy."

"I left them out on purpose for reason I thought even you would be hip enough to understand John. Really, sometimes I think you don't listen to me at all. So, you seem to be calling the shots, so what now brown cow?" Stanley asks.

"We try to see the old lady Birch." John says.

"I knew you were going to say that. Oh, and John..."

"Yes?"

"One other point. I almost hesitate to tell you this. You're so amped up in your conspiracy mode and all."

"What?"

"Well, Barbara said that her boss told her the buyer wanted to know if anyone was inquiring about the letters, under bidders, anybody."

"And what were they supposed to do if someone did inquire?"

"Tell him if anyone was inquiring. Barbara even asked me if it was all right that she told her boss we were inquiring."

"A little tidbit you left out. Nice work 'Columbo,' but then again if indeed something's up, and I think it is…"

"I know you do John."

"Maybe we'll get contacted by the buyer."

"Maybe, or maybe we will develop a shadow."

"Oh come on now. The buyer, whoever that is, has the letters and we don't. So why follow us around? They know the entire contents, not us."

"Barbara said they were true to their word. No copies, but you know John, even if the employees didn't see the letters…"

"Somebody had to." John interrupts.

"Bingo! But who?" Stanley asks.

"Whoever authenticates for the company or whoever wrote the catalog copy had to see the letters."

"I asked about the catalog since it quoted from the letters. I figured what you did; that someone had to have read them. She said only one man writes the copy."

"Who's that?"

"The auction house president," Stanley says.

"Where can we find him?" John asks.

"You really don't think if this big buyer asked them not to share that he would tell us anything meaningful, do you?"

"No, probably not, but shouldn't we leave someone our new address since we've moved hotels, just in case this mysterious buyer wants to reach us?"

"Oh, I see… That's our reason for asking to see the Prez, to leave a forwarding address."

"Exactly…"

"Okay we'll go, but you are still wasting time and money, but for now, I'm sleepy. I just want to watch a little porn and go to sleep," Stanley says.

"Watch porn? Why on Earth would you want to…never mind. I don't want to know. Just get up at 9:00am and meet me in the lobby."

"Okay. Nighty-night John."

"Goodnight Stanley," John says, disappearing back through the adjoining door and into his own room.

Now I'll probably have nightmares of those two humping next door, John thinks just before he lies down and drifts quietly off to sleep.

CHAPTER FIVE

The morning brings rain. Not unusual for Southern California this time of year, but it makes for hateful driving situations as the locals never seem used to it. Wrecks on every highway and byway imaginable make maneuvering a real bitch. What should take minutes can often take hours, and the 101 freeway is one of several that become a large parking lot.

This is why I could never live here, John thinks. *The frustration over traffic alone was enough to drive you crazy.* But he does come often to the city because so much wealth and rare collectibles inevitably pop up there that he really has no choice.

John gets dressed after a quick shower and rings Stanley's room. Getting no answer, he takes the elevator downstairs to the breakfast bar off the main lobby to see if Stanley is waiting for him, which he is.

"You are never on time John," Stanley says as he approaches him.

"Well clearly that's a crock of shit because here I am."

"So now you're upset because I'm on time, is that it?" Stanley asks perturbed.

"Yes, the only thing I should have counted on is that I can't count on you at all."

"It's an endearing quality to some you know," Stanley retorts.

"Really, and who would that be? Alzheimer's victims? People ravaged with A.D.D.?"

"Let's not start the day like this okay?"

"Okay. You eaten yet?" John asks.

"Just some grazing at the breakfast bar. You?"

"No, not hungry. I want to get a jump on all of this. I could barely sleep just thinking about it. Besides, the rain is going to make traffic tough on us."

"Lovely," Stanley says sarcastically. "I thought someone once said that it never rains in Southern California."

"Yes, but the same person said but when it does, it pours."

"Let's go then and get this goose chase over with."

They pick up John's rental car in the downstairs valet, and then start back across town to the auction house offices.

"I feel like a yo-yo. This is our third time going to the same damn dreary building. You know, there are more exciting things to do in L.A. John," Stanley says as they pull back into the underground garage and valet the car again at the auction building.

"Quit your bitching and let's go see this guy," John says.

"How do you know he's here, or will even see us?" Stanley asks.

"Use that charm of yours on 'Miss Sunday Night'."

"Her name is Barbara. Barbara Bain."

John shoots Stanley an amusingly perplexed look. "Are you shittin' me?"

"No, that's her name. Be nice, she's heard all the jokes long before you pal."

"Okay, use your charm on Barbara should you accept this mission."

"I've thought of all the jokes too, Jay Leno, so keep them to yourself."

"I'd love to disavow all knowledge of knowing you," John said continuing the 'Mission Impossible' themed jokes.

"Right back at ya, big boy. I will talk to her again but not for you anymore. I'm doing this so we can put this crap to bed and I can go home. You and I are not making any money John, which is, if you recall, the reason for our little get-together. If this were vacation time for me, I'd be somewhere tropical, not in rain-soaked Los Angeles."

"L.A. usually has nice weather," John says even as it continues to rain outside.

"For budding asthmatics maybe, but not my idea of tropical."

Inside the building, they cross the lobby and John lingers over a magazine stand while Stanley walks up to Barbara's desk.

"Hello," she says, brightening up. "I didn't expect to see you here. Did you come to see me?"

"I wouldn't have missed the opportunity, but my friend here, he's all business you know," he says, pushing his thumb in John's direction. "He still wants to write this story and well, I was hoping you could get us a brief audience with the big guy."

"You aren't going to discuss anything that could get me fired are you?" Barbara says looking panic stricken.

"No, no, I promise pumpkin. You will not even come up in the confab. You have my word on that," Stanley says trying to reassure her.

"Well, okay. I'll see what I can do for you."

Barbara disappears around the corner for a minute or two while Stanley turns back around to face John in the lobby area. He gives him an okay circle sign with his fingers. John just smirks as Stanley thinks, *some people are not happy no matter what you do for them.*

"Yes," Barbara says, suddenly reappearing. "He can see you both but just for a minute though. He's very busy. I told him you want to interview him, and he's a vain bastard, so I thought that may work, but after that it's up to you whether or not he will be any help to you."

"You're the best sweetie!" Stanley kisses her on the cheek. "We're still on for Sunday night aren't we?"

"You bet," she says sweetly smiling.

"Mr. Black," Stanley says as John walks up to them.

"Yes," John says.

"This way please," Stanley replies, looking way too pleased with himself.

John smiles at Barbara as he sails past her and down the hall. "She seemed so sweet," he whispers to Stanley. "I just don't understand it."

"She is sweet John," Stanley whispers back to him.

"Yeah, yeah," he says shaking his head. "What a waste."

"I heard that John. Be nice."

They stop at the end of the long hallway and enter another room through a set of double doors.

"The president does very well for himself," Stanley says as he drinks in the outer office where he and John are asked to wait by another secretary while the president finished with another customer.

"He made time for us though didn't he Stanley?"

"Yes, he did. So what? Barbara said he loves publicity. That's the only reason he made time for us, so don't read anything into it."

"After a sale? No, I'd say he's interested in what we have to say."

"Which is what exactly? That we want to see a copy of a bunch of letters we weren't the winning bidders on and that he promised not to copy in the first place so that we, as journalists I believe it was, can publish the contents, making them valueless to his real bidder and buyer? Oh yeah, he'll jump on that offer," Stanley says sarcastically.

"Of course not," John replies, "We simply ask him if a copy exists. We know it doesn't, he tells us it doesn't, although it will be interesting to hear what excuse he gives. It's that excuse that I want to hear."

"Okay, then what?"

"Then we ask to contact the buyer."

"He will also refuse us that little bit of information. You do realize that don't you, or are you so far gone in your little conspiracy that you're becoming delusional already?"

"True. I agree."

"Then?"

"Then we ask about his procedures and say something like, 'Mr. President, don't you think it's strange that…"

Suddenly, the secretary appears in the doorway. "Mr. Stevens will see you both now. Please come this way."

"Shhh…" John says to Stanley.

"I wasn't the one speaking, so don't you go Shhing me, alright? And if I were speaking, it would be to say, 'In other words, you're winging it," Stanley whispers.

"Uh huh," John says quietly. "Mr. Stevens, how nice of you to take the time to see us," he says, extending his hand. He shakes the president of the auction company's hand firmly as he enters the office a few steps ahead of Stanley.

"Not at all, not at all," says the president meeting his handshake and pumping it firmly. "You said you had some information regarding the sale of Lot 114, the Jim Morrison letters. I would be remiss if I didn't hear what you had to say about such an important lot to us."

"Yes, but it didn't look important in the beginning of your session, did it Mr. Stevens?" John is already on the attack.

"Whatever do you mean by that, Mr. Black?" Mr. Stevens is taken aback by the abruptness of the questioning and is still standing in the middle of the room in front of his desk.

John continues to question Mr. Stevens. "The estimates pre-sale were only ten to fifteen thousand, and in my opinion…"

"Expert opinion," Stanley interrupts with.

"Well yes come to mention it, in my expert opinion, those letters should have fallen in that range, not sold for ten times the amount they did."

Relaxing a little and settling into his own self confidence, Mr. Stevens shrugs his shoulders and almost jokingly says, "Well, we call that a homerun in the auction business Mr. Black. You get two hysterical bidders who, in the heat of the moment, lose their rationale a bit and bid a bit exuberantly. So I take it you were the under bidder and are now experiencing a bit of sour grapes?"

John, realizing he's been caught, regains his composure. "Not at all. I don't have a habit of paying more than something is worth."

"Good for you. Self discipline is important in a live bidding situation, but as the old saying goes, 'an item is worth whatever someone is willing to pay for it'." Mr. Stevens says.

"Yes, yes, but other Morrison letters have been sold, even more important manuscripts such as his poetry and lyrics for far less money."

"Well then we were just lucky I suppose, but you did say you had some news pertinent to the lot Mr. Black. I don't mean to rush you, but I have another appointment waiting." Mr. Stevens was now sounding as if were put off and starts walking around to his desk before sitting down.

"Yes. Yes, of course we did. I mean we do." John looks and Stanley and both men sit down. "My colleague and I are writing a book on the life of Jim Morrison. We have a rather large publishing house behind us, and a six-figure contract. We've been working on the project for two years when we heard from a source of ours that these letters were coming to light and that their content was, well...interesting to say the least. So imagine our surprise when the content was almost all but omitted in the sale, even to qualified bidders during the pre-sale times."

Mr. Stevens shifts in his chair. "Well that is different than our normal policy to be sure, but in this age of copyright and publishing rights, the value of the letters lay in them being unpublished, and the rights were transferred to the winning bidder to publish them. If we just copied them verbatim into our catalog, then they would have been publishable as a news item by any rag that chose to."

"Then there WAS some startling content in the letters?" John asks with his curiosity piqued.

"Not startling, I don't think. I read them."

"So we were told."

Stanley suddenly kicks John in the shin. He takes the strong hint and recovers quickly. "I mean, so we heard."

"Yes well, I write the catalog copy but no one else reads it and as you must have read in the copy I wrote, I simply stated that the letters were very personal and unpublished, a glimpse into his psyche, that kind of poetic prose that helps sell a product with emotion."

"And did so quite well if I may say so," John says while trying to hide his sarcasm.

"Thank you," Mr. Stevens replied smugly.

"Surely something so rare, you kept a copy though. I mean, just between us," John says leaning in and speaking in almost a whisper.

"I often have underbidders wanting copies of documents in sales, so it is our habit not to tempt fate, or our employees I might add, by making something like that available. No copies of these letters exist, not made by us anyway. The consignor assured us she had no copies of them either, nor had they been copied by anyone in all the time they were in her possession, which if I remember correctly, was over 30 years.

"And before that? I mean the letters were older than that according to the dates, which you did release."

"Before that, they had been in a family member's possession, so it's also unlikely to have been copied. If they had, then some past researchers like yourselves would have probably published them by now, don't you think?"

"True enough," John admits.

"So Mr. Black, if a copy was what you expected to secure in this meeting, I'm sorry that I have none to offer, and could not even if I did, as the buyer made the arrangement before winning the lot that no copies could be made for any reason." Mr. Stevens rose to his feet to signal the meeting was ending.

Not satisfied, John tries taunting him. "Do you always do what only a 'prospective buyer' asks of you?"

"Well he had a very fine credit line and made it clear to us early on he expected to pay in his words 'whatever it took to secure them'."

"For what purpose? Did he at least tell you that?"

"That, Mr. Black, was none of my, and may I add your, business," Mr. Stevens says showing a growing impatience.

"But one pays a lot to acquire unpublished material with the hopes of publishing it, doesn't one?"

"Yes I suppose so, but if he is some eccentric who just likes owning rare Morrison letters, who is to say?" Mr. Stevens shrugs his shoulders. "He can do with them as he pleases, now can't he Mr. Black?"

"You are, Mr. Stevens, you are the very one to say!" John says, trying to appeal to his ego and vanity.

"How's that Mr. Black?"

"I mean, excuse me. I mean you will certainly tell us who the lucky bidder was so we may approach them for a copy of the letters? There is no harm in us trying is there? He is certainly allowed to tell us no, but we should hear that from him, unless, of course, you're his designated spokesperson?"

"I can't imagine you'd be successful, Mr. Black, after what I just told you, and NO, I am not in any way the bidder's spokesperson as you say, but unfortunately, our clients are our real value as a company, and we do not give out buyer or seller information to anyone for any reason. Now, if there isn't anything else," he says even more perturbed than before and heading for the door.

"No, nothing else," John says.

"Thank you for the interest in the auction and your bids. We hope you will have the occasion to bid here again." Mr. Stevens watches as both men walk out of the office.

"I'm sure I will. Good day," John says, turning back to shake his hand once again.

"Good day." Mr. Stevens answers, showing them out.

"That accomplished a whole helluva lot of nothing," Stanley says as John and he are leaving the building for the third time in two days.

"Yes I know, but what else can we do? You never know what you may turn up with someone in a conversation. He did seem nervous though, didn't he? Admit that." John surmised.

"No, he seemed pissed off. You wasted his time and lied to get the meeting in the first place. That's all I saw."

"What are you now, Mother Teresa? You lied about who you are to a young woman you slept with to get even more information from."

"Going to sleep with, not slept with," Stanley corrects him. "And I'll keep you posted on that since you keep bringing it up. Why don't we talk about certain ambiguous moral decisions of yours?"

"Glass houses, Stanley. Glass houses," John warns.

"I think that would be great actually. I mean, with glass houses you could see everything going on inside. I could imagine a glass house for those sexy things on that TV series 'Desperate Housewives'. Now that episode I would tune in to watch. I love that little spinner Eva Longoria!"

You're a degenerate, but you know that don't you?" John says sternly.

"And your point is what exactly?"

"Nothing. Absolutely nothing. What the hell does spinner mean anyway, or do I want to know?"

"I will put the term in the glossary of the book I'm writing."

"YOU are writing a book? Shouldn't you read a book first Stan?"

"Cute."

"What, pray tell, is the subject matter of your book?"

"The working title is 'A Bachelor's Guide to Big Game Hunting'."

"Like tigers?"

"Close enough – pussy."

"Cute."

"I'm serious. You've written books on what you know and love, so why shouldn't I?"

"I must admit Stan; it's hard to argue with that kind of logic."

"So, now what, 'Sherlock Homo'?"

"You probably think every guy who isn't banging chicks every night is a homo," John says back to him.

"I don't really think you're a homo John. You know that."

"That's better."

"But 'Sherlock Pathetic' wouldn't have sounded funny now would it?"

"Well Watson, to answer your question, we go and see the consignor."

"For what possible purpose? That's not redundant, that is."

John shoots Stanley a coy look. "I'm hoping her morals lie somewhat closer to yours."

"What's that supposed to mean?"

"Barbara described her as an old lady."

"So…" Stanley quickly caught on to where this was going. "Oh no John, I am not into granny sex. Not even for you to make money, not even to unearth Jim Morrison letters for you."

"No dumb fuck. I mean let's hope she made a copy of those letters even though she was asked not to."

Stanley breathes a sigh of relief. "I'm as hopeful for that as you are. Maybe if you get to read the damn things, you can stop obsessing about all of this. So, how do we find the consignor?"

John looks back to the auction house. "Maybe we stake out the place hoping your information is right about this old woman appearing for her money today."

"Barbara, I mean, 'Deep Throat', is a good source. Not to worry."

"Cute."

"Just trying to make you smile John. Really, lighten up. We'll stalk the granny person like you want. God forbid you don't get your way. You're not worth living with." Stanley says as they drive out onto the street.

They pull their car into a Gulf service station directly across the street from the auction house and park over by the air and water pumps before turning off the engine.

After a few minutes of sitting quietly, Stanley speaks. "This is like a stake out huh John."

John knows Stanley is only poking fun at him and the situation. "Shut up and keep your eyes peeled for this woman."

"I don't have to."

"Really?" John asks surprised. "And why the hell not?"

"Barbara said she would give my cell phone a jingle whenever the Birch woman hits the lobby. Seems she has to go upstairs to get her check from the president's secretary. So we'll have time to follow her when she leaves the building."

"And you just now decided to mention that fact to me?"

"You looked so happy in your 'James Bond' mode and all that I didn't want to bother you 'Double O Zero'."

"That's fine. I'm hungry. Let's go get something to eat then if you're sure Barbara will call you. You are sure, right?"

"Uh, yep, I'm sure but I don't think we'll have time to eat."

"Why not?"

"Look." Stanley points across the street to a little old lady walking up the sidewalk into the building.

"You think that's her? She could be anyone. Did Barbara describe her to you?"

"No, but how many little old ladies do you think they were expecting today John? The auction is over. You know we were the only customers in the building in the past hour."

"True, older people are more likely to be sellers than buyers at that stage of their life."

"How very informative! I can't believe The Discovery Channel hasn't beaten down your door to do a show with you by now."

Despite Stanley's flippant remark, John says, "Me either." He then proceeds to flip Stanley the middle finger.

"Now that's not even trying. I know you're more clever than that."

"Eat me."

"Oh much better, and a visual too! You've just given up then have you?" Suddenly Stanley's cell phone rings. As he goes to answer it, they see the little old lady leaving again by the lobby doors.

"Damn, she's a fast one for her age, I'll give her that," John says. "If that's her."

Stanley answers his cell phone. "Hello…" Hearing Barbara on the other end, he begins a conversation. "Well hello my love. What's that? Oh good. I was worried you were calling to break our date," he says as he motions for John to follow the older woman getting into a late model blue Buick that's sitting on the street by a meter box.

He points and nods his head for the sake of indication. "Oh she did, did she? Just now? Oh that is too bad. You're right, we will never make it back that fast, but thanks for trying honey. See you tomorrow night," he says and then makes a kissing sound into the phone.

"I think I need a shot of insulin," John whispers as he turns their car around to follow the older woman. He nods and rolls his eyes in acknowledgement when Stanley whispers "Don't lose her."

Turning his attention back to his phone call, Stanley continues talking to Barbara. "Thanks. No, that's okay hon. I appreciate you trying."

"Trying what, or should I ask?" John asks as Stanley hangs up his phone.

"That's the problem with sexual repression cases like you John. Sex is always on your mind and John, that's not healthy."

"Whatever."

"She said that she was sorry she couldn't call sooner or keep her around in time for us to get there. She doesn't know your obsession had us lurking across the street. I don't share everything with her John. It would scare her away. That's why I suggested we wait around the old lady's appointment time. Smart huh John? Come on, admit it," he says nudging him in the ribs.

"Okay, okay. Good job. Now stop elbowing me while I'm driving!"

"Sorry you doubted me now?" Stanley asks smugly.

"Yes, yes, alright."

"Damn. She drives so slow," Stanley observes, "we might still be able to grab that bite to eat."

"Do you know an old lady who doesn't drive slowly?"

"Yes."

"Who?"

"The little old lady from Pasadena."

John throws him an 'I can't believe you said that' look. "And do the 18-year-olds you prey upon understand you when you make 'Beach Boys' song references to them?"

"YOU actually also qualify. You drive fairly fast for a little old lady."

"I do not, and I'm also not an old lady!"

"All in the eye of the beholder, I suppose. Just keep following her, and for goodness sake, don't get caught John."

"You think 'Grandma Moses' here is going to get suspicious?"

"Maybe."

"Stanley, this is probably the first time anyone has followed her since she welcomed home the troops in '44. I bet I could pull into her driveway without spooking her, so just relax."

They pull into an older subdivision off a main street, where after viewing the houses, Stanley makes the observation, "Nice neighborhood, it was back when Edison lived here I mean."

"You're such a snob Stanley."

"No I'm not, but why keep up a house payment if your house is no bigger than an apartment anyway? It's a bad investment. That's all I'm saying."

"Pride of ownership would be a reason, and having your lifelong friends around you."

"Are you even looking out your window at these old dumps, or listening to me when I speak John?" Stanley asks with a sound of disgust in his voice.

They pull their car over just down the street when they see Birch pull into a driveway and up under a carport.

"Okay, just so we don't spook her, let's wait a few minutes and then go up and ring the bell," John suggests.

"Okay, but don't wait too long. She could doze off on us you know." Stanley jokes.

CHAPTER SIX

After about 15 minutes, the two walk up the street and head for her front door. She has an intercom-style doorbell, which John rings once. He also presses the buzzer button on the plate beneath her name – Hazel Birch.

"I just knew it would be Hazel or Bertha or Eleanor, you know…" Stanley remarks.

"Cause you were expecting maybe what? Candy or Alicia?"

A voice coming over the intercom interrupts their banter. "Yes?"

John thinks fast and starts speaking into the box. "Hello. My name is Eric Carmen, and I'm with…"

"I don't want anything," she says in the middle of his sentence. "The sign says 'No Soliciting' you know.

"She has spunk, I'll give her that." Stanley whispers.

John keeps up with his persona. "Oh yes ma'am, I know. I'm not a salesman. Me and Mr. uh, Steinman here, we are from C&R Auctions."

"Who?"

"C&R Auctions. We got your name from the auction house where you consigned and sold some Jim Morrison letters recently."

"Oh, wait just a minute." She opens the door still leery, peering out past a still fastened old chain lock. "You boys look nice," she says as more of an assessment than anything else.

"Thank you. Mrs. Birch, is it?

"Yes, but how did you know my name?" she asks.

"Hello. Like I was saying, the auction house told us of your great consignment of the Jim Morrison letters recently."

"Yes. I just came from there in fact," she says, "but I told them I don't have any other letters if that's what you boys want, and please tell your auction house the same, but thank you anyway," she says, starting to close the door.

"Oh no, we understand there are no more, but we represent the under bidder at the sale of your letters."

"The what?" she asks.

"This is going to be tougher than I thought," Stanley whispers to John.

John attempts to explain. "The under bidder is the person who had the bid just one increment under the winning bid." He ignores Stanley's remark entirely.

"Oh I see, but how could I help you or them?" Mrs. Birch asks.

"Well Mrs. Birch, we got an exciting offer from the under bidder. He was willing to pay you a great deal of money for just a copy of the letters you sold."

"What?!" hisses Stanley. "Not our money! We're not..." he whispers at John, who completely ignores him, but steps down hard on his foot.

"Why would only a copy be worth so much?" Mrs. Birch asks.

"Well, our client represents a publishing house writing a book on Mr. Morrison's life and understood that the content of the letters was remarkable."

"Remarkable? I don't think that's the case," she says.

"Well interesting to Jim Morrison fans anyway."

"I think it was all just babbling if you ask me."

John takes a chance, asking, "May we come in and discuss it further with you?"

Mrs. Birch thinks about it for a few seconds and says, "Well, I suppose so." She slides the chain off the lock and motions for them to come inside.

John surveys the living room they've just entered. "What a lovely home you have."

"Thank you." She turns to them and asks, "Would you two like something to drink?"

"No thank you, Mrs. Birch." John replies.

"Well do please sit down."

The trio sits down on two chairs and a couch in the living room while John continues speaking. "So like I was starting to ask you before, do you have a copy we may negotiate the sale of for you?"

"No. I was told not to make a copy of the letters by the auction house. I'm surprised they didn't tell you that."

"Me too," Stanley adds, glaring at John who continues to ignore him.

"Who told you that? I mean, who at the auction house told you not to copy the letters Mrs. Birch?"

"Mr. Stevens at the auction house."

"Oh yes. The President of the auction company."

"Yes."

"Did he tell you why he'd said not to copy them?"

Mrs. Birch nods her head. "He said they had a man who was very interested in the sale and would be buying them no matter what the price got up to, and he said whenever that happened they would be sure the main paid dearly, and I would make a lot of money."

"And them as well I imagine."

"Yes, they got 20% commission you know."

"Yes, I know." John sounds innocent as he says, "How could they make him pay dearly. I wonder..."

Mrs. Birch appears to be in total agreement. "You know, I thought about that too. I think they knew whatever amount he was willing to pay and probably bid him up to that amount. I felt terrible about that part, but Mr. Stevens told me that's just the auction game these days."

"Indeed. He did, huh?" John's curiosity is rising. "And do you remember how soon after the sale was announced it was that he asked you about not copying the letters and all of the rest of this?"

"I don't know. About three weeks after I suppose."

"Hadn't you made a copy of the letters, just for yourself in all these years?"

"No. I kept the letters, a dear friend left them to me you know, in my safe deposit box at the bank with a bunch of papers. Actually, I thought I had thrown them out years ago, but stumbled across them one day doing some insurance business after my George died." Off of John's and Stanley's confused expressions, Mrs. Birch adds, "George was my husband. 53-years married..." she says, her voice trailing off quietly.

"I see," John says, lowering his head a bit to pause before pressing on. "Well you had read them though surely?"

"Oh yes! Once years and years ago, and then again recently when I got them from the bank's deposit box. They didn't make any more sense to me now than they did years ago," she says, chuckling to herself.

"What did the letters say exactly? I mean, Mr. Stevens said not to copy them, but he didn't say you couldn't discuss what you read, right?"

"No, I suppose not. You two boys work for the same business as he does, right?"

"Correct."

Mrs. Birch hesitates. "He did ask me not to do any interviews about them though."

John continues pressing her. "Okay, but since we are in the same business he is, then we're not breaking any trust, now are we? What were they about?"

"Oh they were just some letters he wrote back home to his mother."

"His mother?" John queries.

"Yes. She was a dear, sweet friend of mine until her death and she gave me the letters from her son. Jimmy, she called him."

"Do you know why she kept these out of all his letters to her?"

"Oh, I don't think he wrote her that much. Usually he phoned her, I believe. They weren't always close you know."

"No, I didn't know that," John says sounding interested.

"She kept these for sentimental reasons. I believe because they were the last time she heard from him before he died of that awful drug overdose."

"What was the gist of the letters then?"

"Well, they said he was going to stay in Paris for a while with his girlfriend, and that he was real worried that someone was out to harm him if I remember correctly."

"That's important though isn't it, in the light of his death ultimately. So young and all I mean. Didn't you find that interesting?" John asks Mrs. Birch.

"Well if was someone else maybe so, but his mother told me he did drugs and was paranoid a lot of the time. Always talking about the government and war and all those hippie causes they had back then."

"Who did he think was trying to harm him? Did he say?"

Mrs. Birch shakes her head. "He didn't say, but he thought that some person was following him and that person was somehow involved in the deaths of Jimi Hendrix and Janis Joplin."

"They were killed?" John asks incredulously.

"Of course not. That's what I mean. Like his mother told me, it was pure fiction. He wrote fiction and poetry too you know. His mother thought that this was just some other fiction he was working on writing."

"She didn't show them to anyone when he died suddenly?"

"No, whatever for?"

"Yes, I guess you're right." John looks to Stanley and back to her. "Did she ever copy the letters?"

"I don't think so. She kept them in a shoe box under her bed with some baby stuff."

The collector side of John comes in to play as he asks, "What kind of baby stuff?"

"Oh…she had a tooth of his as a baby, some pictures, and a lock of his hair."

"What happened to those things?"

"I don't know to be honest with you."

"Oh, I thought she willed all of her things to you."

She shook her head again. "Oh no, I wasn't in her will. She gave me the letters while she was still alive."

"Why do you think she gave them to you while she was still alive?"

"She said reporters and book writers and all were always looking for stuff he'd written, and she couldn't bear to see them sold or out there. She thought the letters would make him look, well, you know…sick in the head during his final days. She had a break in at her home a couple of times, which was the last straw for her. She didn't want thieves finding anything of his. She said she made a lot of money as one of the interests in his music after he died and I think she had lawyers always advising her to protect his name and image as best she could."

Not necessarily wanting to make her feel uncomfortable, John asks, "Forgive me, but why did you sell them? If she didn't want them, why not destroy them since she didn't want them published or sold to the public?"

Mrs. Birch looks down at her lap and then back up at John and Stanley. She's clearly feeling guilty about her transaction, but tries to explain. "I feel terrible about that part of all of this, I really do, but one day I looked at them and I didn't think they made him look so bad. She had passed away, and Jim was remembered as a hippie who did drugs and overdosed anyway. I really needed the money for a nurse. I need around the clock care these days and I thought it was a waste to not sell them when I found out they were worth money." She shifts in her chair. "I'd read in the newspaper one day that some letters of Janis Joplin had brought $8,000.00. Of course, I had no idea these would sell as high as they did, but that's what set me to thinking of selling them."

"No, I should think not," John says while shooting a look to Stanley, who rolls his eyes at him.

"Well, there is even more money in it for you Mrs. Birch...if you should remember a copy lying about. Medical expenses are so high these days. It's a crime, isn't it Stanley?"

"Oh, don't get me started on what is and isn't a crime," Stanley pointedly says.

"Well..." she starts.

"Yes?" John says while almost tipping over in his chair from excitement.

"I did copy one letter, but only one of them."

"Why is that?"

"Originally the auction houses competed for my consignment."

"Houses?" John asks.

"Sure. I sent a letter detailing what I had to two auction companies at first, in case one didn't care for the letters."

"Both here in Los Angeles?"

"Yes," she answers. "So I copied the first letter and placed it in each envelope and told them I had several letters written at the same time. Originally I call them, but they said they'd need to see them to authenticate that it really was Jim Morrison's handwriting."

"Of course," John agrees.

"So that's how I offered them. Gray's Auctions showed the most interest and offered me estimates of ten to fifteen thousand, but the other auction house said they thought they'd sell for less I went with Mr. Stevens at C&R Auctions."

"Sensible," Stanley interjects. "Sensible…"

"You have a copy of that letter then?" John asks her.

"Yes, it's still at the bank."

"Why at the bank?"

"Well, I had them make the copies for me and I put the letters back into the safe deposit box."

"Oh," John says, looking a bit deflated until Mrs. Birch continued with her explanation.

"So I made two more copies of it and left them there in case I would have to send more offers to more auction companies. Then Mr. Stevens told me not to make any copies. I thought one day I would destroy them when I got back to the bank again."

Their conversation is interrupted when Mrs. Birch's telephone rings. "Excuse me," she says, getting up and walking over to it. She answers it in the kitchen, just barely out of ear shot of Stanley and John.

While she's out of the room, John turns to Stanley and asks, "Do you think we can entice her to show up the bank copy at least?"

"I hope so for your sake or this is all a waste of time, like the auction and the visit to the president, and..."

"Okay, okay, I get it..."

As usual, thinking with his wallet, Stanley looks at John. "Let me ask you a question sport. Is there any money in us having the copy of this letter?"

"No Stanley. You know, everything is not always about money."

"In your world maybe..." Stanley mutters as Mrs. Birch returns to the living room.

"When it rains, it pours. They say very good luck is always coupled with some bad luck," she says.

"Yes it does sometimes seem that way. Are you okay Mrs. Birch?" John asks.

"Oh, I'm fine, just terribly old. No, that was my insurance adjuster. My home was broken into a couple weeks back you know."

"REALLY!" John exclaims.

Oh God, here we go, Stanley thinks to himself.

John shoots another knowing look to Stanley, who smiles weakly.

Mrs. Birch starts to reminisce. "Yes, I remember when this neighborhood was top rate, but that was a very long time ago I'm afraid. In fact, that's another reason, my safety that I want to move into a retirement village. They have security you know. It's very nice there."

John is fully interested in her story. "Did they do any harm to you or steal anything when they broke in?"

"No. Probably just kids. That's what the police thought because they just made a mess of everything."

"What do you mean a mess?"

"You know, emptied drawers on the floor, cushions on my sofa were all ripped up, just a hateful bunch of hooligans doing vandalism."

"Have you ever heard of anyone else's home in your neighborhood being broken into Mrs. Birch?"

"Well, yes, over the years a few people's houses have been broken into. A friend of mine lost her jewelry and another lost some money he had hidden in his sofa."

"Cliché I suppose, to hide money under a mattress. I guess everyone knows to look there, right?" John smiles at his joke. "But nothing was stolen from you?"

"No, but I don't own anything of value really."

"Well, I couldn't help but notice the figurines in that glass case on the wall. Aren't many of them made of ivory?" John gestures to a tall étagère filled with various sized figurines, all intricately carved from ivory and Oriental looking in nature.

"Yes, yes they are. My you have a good eye for things like that."

"Yes, he used to," Stanley sarcastically interjects, which John completely ignores.

"My late husband bought those nearly 40 years ago on trips abroad for his company. I suppose they are valuable, but I could never sell them because of the sentimental reasons."

"No jewelry was stolen then?"

"I only own what I wear and I had it all on me at the time."

"When did it occur? The break-in, I mean."

"In the middle of the day about three weeks ago."

"Aren't you usually home then?"

"Yes, usually, but I had left for a doctor's appointment."

He's starting to actually sound like 'Columbo', Stanley muses to himself as John continues his line of questioning.

"How long were you gone?"

"Oh, I guess a few hours."

"How lucky for them," John says looking back at Stanley for a reaction.

"Pardon me?" Mrs. Birch sounds almost injured by John's remark.

He recovers quickly. "I mean how lucky for you not to be home. You might have been harmed."

"Yes, quite lucky. I felt the same way."

Getting back to the topic at hand, John takes a breath and asks, "So about the copy of the one letter…may we see it?"

"Well...I suppose if you wanted to come to the back with me, I could let you look at it, but I don't want to anger the man who paid all that money for the lot of them, so I really couldn't let you copy it."

"No, no, that's all right. I just wanted to read one for research."

"Research, yes. For your book, right?"

"Yes," John replies.

"Well, that's alright I suppose."

"When may we go?" John asks, being a bit pushier this time.

"Well we could go now if you don't mind taking me. I already drove once today, to the auction house in fact."

"Really?" Stanley feigns surprise at her statement.

"Yes and my eyes aren't really what they should be. I'd feel better if you boys could take me. Do you mind?"

"No, not at all..." John says with smile across his face.

"Would you mind stopping at a pharmacy long enough for me to pick up a prescription as well?" she asks.

"No, that would be our pleasure. Right Stanley?" John says, looking at him sternly.

"Uh huh," Stanley says rolling his eyes at John.

John cuts him a sharp look to stop as the dynamic duo follows Mrs. Birch as she locks up her house and goes out to the driveway. John headed for his rented Cadillac, but Mrs. Birch stops him.

"Oh I wouldn't impose further by asking you to use up your gas. It's crazy what gas costs these days. I meant for you to drive my car."

John smiles at her gracious offer. "Well, that's very thoughtful of you, but as reporters, we get to write off any gas purchases as a tax expense, so let's take my car. You'll be more comfortable in it, and I think since you're doing us the favor, we shouldn't be using up your gas."

"Well...if you're quite sure..."

"Oh yes, quite," John says as they make their way to the Cadillac. Their first stop is the pharmacy, after which they eventually arrive at Mrs. Birch's bank. It was a small neighborhood bank, not yet owned by the larger conglomerates.

Not wanting to miss the chance at getting on Stanley's nerves, John whispers, "Looks like you guys missed one."

Stanley rolls his eyes as they pull into the parking lot of the bank. "We will eventually get them all you know John. That's the very definition of world dominance you know."

"What do you mean?" asks Mrs. Birch upon hearing Stanley's comment.

Realizing he wasn't acting like a journalist and was overheard by Mrs. Birch, Stanley quickly improvises. "I mean a good reporter will always get his story. Like we are...thanks to you, of course." He smiles at her.

"Well I hope it helps. I really still don't see a story here though boys."

"I know what you mean," Stanley says giving a glaring look to John who ignores him again.

Once inside the bank, Mrs. Birch wanders over to Customer Service and shows her ID card and signs in to gain access to her safety deposit box. The three are ushered into a small room where the bank employee leaves the box on a small table and closes the door, leaving them alone. "Just ring that bell," the employee says while pointing to a buzzer, "when you are ready to return the box to the safe. Will you need a bag or container of any kind Mrs. Birch?"

"Oh no," she says, "just looking up some old papers. Won't be long at all."

The employee excuses herself from the three of them as Mrs. Birch opens her box. She takes out a large manila envelope and hands it to John.

"Thank you," John says smiling as he opens the envelope and slides out some paper. He begins to read the top sheet.

CHAPTER SEVEN

It was a copy as she had said of a handwritten letter on plain lined paper and at once he realized that it was in fact, the handwriting of Jim Morrison. Trying to hide his excitement, he reads the opening lines of the letter.

"This whole thing has me sobered up Mom. No drink for your boy. No more, I promise you that. I don't want to end up like them. I believe more than anyone in what they were doing. Live and let live, you know, but now, I think they want to try and shut me up too Momma. They say what happened in Miami was against the establishment.

"Christ Momma. I dropped my pants because I was so freaking smashed and the crowd was pushing for something like that Momma. It was like one big party. I thought it would be funny and something to get press on, not some social statement that they made it out to be. Those people paid to see me and it felt private. I didn't think I'd be arrested over it. They must think I will overdo it and die from drugs and rock n' roll too, but not me Momma, no way. I swear. I told a press dude at Rolling Stone Magazine a few weeks ago I'd never go out that way and I won't, and I want you to believe me on that but, all this crap is bigger than me and I'm scared and a little depressed. But I write better when I'm down Ray says, and a lot of artists do well when they suffer for their art, but I think I've pissed off the wrong people Momma.

"So tell the fan club president for me that I'm okay here and not going to break up The Doors like the press think. Tell them I'm moving on to new stuff that I think the fans will really dig.

"But I don't know who to trust anymore with any information, which is why I'm writing you Momma. I think they got to Jimi and Janis, Momma, and ever since I've been here, I can't shake the feeling that I'm being followed by some dude.

"Pray for me Momma. I know you always have.

"Love, Jimmy

The page has a hastily written P.S. on it as well.

"Momma, I don't want to scare you, but I will write again every few weeks and if you don't hear from me, you will know something's gone wrong.

"Love, Jimmy"

John slowly puts the letter back into the envelope. "Thank you, Mrs. Birch." He hands it back to her. "I really appreciate your having let me read the letter. You say the other letters were similar?"

"They were the same rantings Mr. Carmen. Like I told you, it's nothing special. You know people who do drugs and abuse alcohol always get paranoid and feel like everyone's out to get them," she says disapprovingly.

"Yes I suppose that could explain it," John replies. "Just a very odd coincidence though. His death coming so soon after these letters, or hadn't you thought of that?"

"Well, yes, I suppose so, but to be extremely frank Mr. Carmen…"

"Please call me Eric."

"Of course, Eric, his mother once told me she expected a call most any day that her Jimmy was dead. It didn't really come as a complete shock to her, although don't get me wrong, I'm sure she prayed that he get help, but God bless him, he obviously never did."

"No."

"A real waste," she comments.

Knowing that their time at the bank was over, John rises from his chair and says, "Thank you again for letting us read this one anyway. Would you like to go anywhere else or just back home Mrs. Birch?"

"Back home please. My stories are starting soon."

"Stories?" John asks.

"Her soap operas," Stanley explains.

"Yes. Which do you watch Mr. Steinman?" she asks turning to look at Stanley.

"Oh no, I just meant to explain to Eric here…"

John shoots a strange look at Stanley and says, "Yes, which do you watch?" He smirks with amusement.

"My mother used to be addicted to them and called them stories too." Stanley then looks at John, who is still smirking at him. "Don't look at me like I'm pathetic."

The three of them climb back into the rented Cadillac and head south down the main street in the direction of Mrs. Birch's home. John is a little slow to notice that they'd picked up a tail. Just before turning into the older subdivision that Mrs. Birch and her friends live in, John notices the car behind him has not changed once since leaving the bank.

"Uh, Jim…" he says to Stanley.

"Yes Eric?" he says back in a smart manner.

"We have a friend."

"Yes we certainly do!" Stanley says. "Mrs. Birch here couldn't be sweeter if she was dipped in honey." He pats her on the back of her shoulder from the back seat where he sits.

"You have no ageism, I'll give you that," John whispers, "but I meant behind us," he says thumbing behind him with his right hand.

Stanley looks over his shoulder. "Oh…"

"You couldn't use a mirror?" John asks, perturbed.

"Well I'm sorry Eric. They don't have side mirrors for the people in the back seat," he whispers back.

"Or maybe you could've taken my word for it," John hisses back in a whisper.

"Then you shouldn't have motioned at me like that."

Now aware of their whispered tones, Mrs. Birch becomes concerned. "What's the matter Mr. Carmen?"

"Oh nothing. I just think I recognize the car behind us from back at the bank."

"Oh, probably just someone who lives here like me and uses the same bank. A lot of my friends use it because it's so close."

"Yes I'm sure that's it, Mrs. Birch."

"Who else could it be? You look so concerned."

John tries covering his concern with a flimsy explanation. "In the field of investigative reporting, our, uh…competitors often follow us for leads and the like, you know."

Having taken a liking to her two escorts, Mrs. Birch says, "Well, I'll tell you what I'll do. I promise not to show anyone else the letter until you tell me that it's okay and your book is ready."

John smiles at her graciousness. "That's very sweet of you, and you know sometimes these guys can be pretty uh...rough, I mean persistent. So I think for your own sake, you might want to not even tell anyone the letter existed. Just stick to the story that the auction house is telling everyone – that you never had a copy and don't remember much of the contents."

"Well, I'm sure you are being a little too concerned for me, but okay, if you say so. You both were so nice to me, and to take me to the pharmacy. I will do what you ask."

"Great!" And if anyone were to ask who we were, just tell them we were looking for the letters or copies but you told us there weren't any and we left."

"Okay Mr. Carmen, anything you say."

As Mrs. Birch gets out of the car, the blue sedan races quickly around them, swerving right across the corner and past them. *Damn tinted glass*, John thinks while trying to look at the driver. He walks Mrs. Birch up the walk and sees her inside.

"Here's my card Mrs. Birch. Should you need to reach me, that's my cell phone and we will probably be around Los Angeles for a few more days. If anything...strange comes up, or you need my help in any way, don't hesitate to call me."

"You're both so sweet. Yes, I will keep your card, thank you." She looks down at the card and then back to John with a look of confusion. "It says John Black on it. Who is that, Mr. Carmen?"

Covering quickly, John replies, "Oh, that's my assistant. He'll know how to reach me. I ran out of my own personal cards."

"Oh I see. Okay then, goodbye, and please say goodbye to that nice boy Mr. Steinman outside for me would you."

"I will, and thanks again Mrs. Birch. You've been more help than you realize."

"That's nice of you to say," she says while closing her door.

"Well..." Stanley hisses as soon as John gets into the driver's seat. "I suppose you think you're right about all of this as usual?"

"I am right that something's not right about all of this."

"You think her break-in has something to do with it don't you? Admit it, you do!"

"Yes, I do. It's too coincidental."

"What, may I ask were the thieves looking for?"

"I don't think they were thieves. I think it's the buyer wanting to ensure that no more letters or copies of letters were lying about."

"And you really think that car was following us, and if so, this all has to do with those letters?" Stanley asks.

"Yes I do. Not the letters, per se, but our inquiries about the letters. And you said yourself that Barbara told the president of the auction house, who notified only one person of our interest."

"The buyer..."

"Exactly!"

"So, was there anything Earth-shattering in the letter you read at the bank?"

John nods his head yes. "He was writing his mother like Mrs. Birch told us."

"Which we already knew. The auction catalog told us that John."

"Yeah, yeah, hold your horses. In it, he says that he is scared that someone had been following him. So he left for Paris for a while as a break, but that he thinks someone in Paris is following him. He said his apartment was not safe and that he planned on moving under an alias somewhere else. He thinks they may be police of some kind or the mob doing the following, and thinks that they had something to do with Janis' and Jimi's deaths as well. He thinks the reason is because he was so outspoken against war and all that hippie agenda stuff that was going on at the time, and get this! He said he would write her every three weeks and if she didn't get a letter, it would be because something happened to him!"

Trying to make sense of what he's being told, Stanley asks, "So why wouldn't 'Mama Morrison', after a letter like that, do something?"

"She probably told her friend. Remember, she also thought her son overdosed and had substance abuse problems."

"Doesn't history remember it that way?" Stanley asks.

"No, not exactly. In fact, in doing a little research on the web, many of his friends said he was a lush in the bottle a lot of the time, but that drugs weren't his bag. He is quoted as stating that anyone who lost their lives to drugs was a loser."

"So you really believe that the government – OUR government – rubbed out some drugged out hippie rock star because of his lifestyle?"

"Not because of his lifestyle. Even Sir Paul McCartney was deported briefly for marijuana possession. Do you recall that Stanley?"

"Well yes, kind of iconic now that it's legal to use marijuana."

"It is not legal to possess marijuana Stanley."

"It is too John, to help your vision. Shows what you know."

"Medical marijuana for vision problems like Mrs. Birch there is different than being widespread legal for everyone to tote around. Paul McCartney never even wore glasses, so there goes your reasoning." John looks at his driving companion. "Do you really think marijuana possession is legal Stanley? Do I need to check your pockets before letting you in my car again?"

"No."

"My point is…"

"Oh, you had a point?" Stanley snidely asks.

"Yes. My point is those were turbulent, war torn and politically unstable times for this country. People were dying in Vietnam. Today even most people aren't sure why."

"Kinda like the Gulf War?"

"Well yes, in that people aren't sure why we're there, if that's what you mean."

"We've been warring in that gulf for a while now. You think the gulf is winning John? What the hell is a gulf anyway?"

Not believing what he's hearing, John looks at Stanley. "Are you okay? I mean, did you hit your head while I was inside or something. Really?"

"I just like saying the word "gulf" to be honest with you."

"As I was saying," John continues perturbed, "There were these rich young singers singing protest songs, inciting riots in the youth concerning a war they never even fought in."

"Like the gulf war?"

"Stop it!"

"Okay, okay."

"Singing out civil liberties, freedoms of speech. Maybe that holds up for you and me, but when someone has a mass following of impressionable people, they need to show some sense of responsibility."

"You really believe that John?"

"Yes," John says defiantly.

"Well then, where were you on the night each of them 'died'?"

"Oh now I'm a suspect? A little too young, I'm afraid. Can't make it that easy for you buddy. I was only showing the other side of the coin that may have cost them their lives. It's a dangerous thought Stanley;

when people begin to feel they need to teach a generation a lesson in social responsibility."

"Well even if any of this matters or amounts to a hill of beans, what can we do forty years after the fact? You don't have the letters, don't have but in your head the content of one letter, and don't know where they are either. No judge in his right mind would force the buyer's identity."

"Why not?" John asks defensively.

"They'd point out that you were a bidder, and an unsuccessful one at that. Sour grapes anyway, that's what I would do if I were a judge."

"And you think there's no way your new girl will get us his identity?"

"Like I said, she doesn't even know it and the president ain't talking to us again. You probably agree on that point, yes?"

"Yes, yes, reluctantly, but yes."

"So where do that leave us John? A big fat nowhere, that's where. Are you satisfied now? Please say you are John," Stanley pleads with him.

As if he's not listening at all, John says, "What if we held a press conference or made it a news bit?"

"What? Why?"

"For two reasons. First, to see if it drives out any more information, and for a second reason…"

"Which is?" Stanley asks.

"To protect us in case someone is after us."

Stanley tries using a bit of deductive reasoning of his own. "Why would anyone do that? Come after us I mean. Hasn't the statute of limitations run out on Morrison if he was killed? Besides, why would anyone care that we had a crackpot theory that he was murdered? We wouldn't be the first you know."

"True. In fact, some people think he faked his death and is still alive."

"Yes and those same idiots see Elvis pumping gas at every quickie mart they go to as well."

"Yes I know, just wishful thinking on the part of the fans, but listen, there is some credible evidence for foul play of some kind like this is starting to look like."

"How's that?"

"No one but Pamela Courson, his girlfriend, saw his body after he died, but in one account she called a friend of Jim's to come over. There are conflicting reports on whether he was DOA or if an ambulance responded, and other weird inconsistencies too. Like how he was cremated, which was not his wish, and there was no open coffin service held before the cremation. And, don't forget Pamela herself thought something was odd about it all, although her story, to be fair, has changed often over the years, and while it's true that part is puzzling, let's not forget she was behind some of the push to the fans to make them believe he may still be alive."

"So you think the murderers killed her for stating things contrary to his murder? Come on John, you're really reaching now."

"I didn't say I had all the answers."

"Yes, but do you have any of the answers?"

"Maybe the murderer pressured her into the 'Jim is alive' story to take the heat off of him or them. Did you ever think of that?"

"Or her…let's not be sexist. As long as you're dreaming all this crap up… So now what John? You're still calling the shots it would seem."

"Glad you're on board buddy."

"I'm not on board, just rubbernecking like you do at a really bad accident in the middle of the highway."

How nice, with imagery and all! Okay let's see. Now I think next we go to Paris and see if our investigations turn up anything in the 'City of Lights'."

"Paris? As in France? What the…?"

"Can you think of any other place to go next that may actually yield any new information?"

"Not off the top of my head, but this is a Rome, Georgia, you know. Nice Southern girls, warm weather, but Paris, France, John? You don't think this trail is a bit cold to be going over there?"

"Not really. You know what I actually think?"

"I can't wait to hear."

"That it's heating up a bit."

"Oh really, that's a little smug even for you. You want to tell me why you think that things are 'heating up' as you put it?"

John peers into his rear-view mirror while continuing to talk. "Because that nice blue sedan with the tinted windows is behind us again."

Stanley looks in the right side mirror. "Damn, I think you're right."

"I know I'm right, but don't be so worried."

"I'm not worried."

"Why'd you say damn then?"

"'Damn' was because you may be right, your idea that is, but I have a better idea."

"What's that?"

"Dropping it altogether now that someone is following us."

"No."

"I thought you'd say that. I like Paris John, but need I remind you that you're the one who hates to fly?"

"I know. I'll need you to get me some Xanax again."

"I'm not going down like Rush Limbaugh for you John!"

"Shut up! I know you still have some."

"I do not. Your information is faulty."

"Really?"

"Yes. Besides, how would you know something like that?"

"I was bored waiting for your date so I rifled through your toiletry bag in the hotel."

"Nothing is sacred to you is it John? You act like you're my wife. Sometimes it's...unsettling, is what it is."

"So is this car. He's still behind us. If I speed up or slow down he stays, matching us no matter what I do. Any idea of what we should do?"

"I'm not your pimp or your drug dealer John."

"So you don't care that we're still being followed? Okay, get me a Xanax or I'll hold your arm for the entire eleven hours on the plane until all the blood drains out of it."

"Okay, I'll get you a Xanax, but John..."

"Yes?"

"You know Jim Morrison would probably not agree."

"Agree to what?"

"You having to get high to come and check on him."

"Shut up…"

Stanley, smirking and chuckling silently continues to taunt John. "Okay, okay. Whatever gets the itch out of your ass, John. I'm all for that now, but what about our little tail? Do you think they'll come all the way to Paris with us John?"

"I hope not, but I truly don't know." John considers his travel options. "Well, I don't think it's wise to go back to the hotel. It's getting dark so let's see how far they'll really go to keep following us."

At the next light, John starts to move forward but suddenly slams on the brakes. The driver of the car following them is caught off guard and slams on his brakes, narrowly missing the Cadillac by swerving to the side.

John rolls down the window and motions for the car behind them to come around. He turns on the Cadillac's hazard lights. The blue Buick behind them stays where it is for a moment and then speeds quickly around the Cadillac. Stanley and John look at the car as it speeds off. Both of them have observed the Buick's license plates and realize their significance.

Stanley says, "Holy crap, John!"

"I know. I saw them too. Did you make out any of the numbers?"

"No, I was too stunned that they were government plates."

"Me too," John answers.

"You see anything else?"

"No. You?"

"No."

"John, you as usual, are pissing off all the wrong people by staying around Los Angeles right now."

"I agree with you."

Thoroughly surprised at his admission, Stanley looks at John. "You do?"

"I do...so let's go to Paris."

"I was afraid that's what you'd say," Stanley says as the smile starts to disappear. "Alright, let's go to Paris."

John grins with the satisfaction of knowing he's talked Stanley into heading for Paris. Putting the Cadillac back into gear, he swings a u-turn at the nearest light. The GPS system, previously programmed for the hotel trip back responds to the change in course. "Make a legal u-turn in one block," it says in a mechanical yet feminine voice.

"Why is she talking again? This one is damn chatty." Stanley complains.

"We still had it programmed for the hotel and now we aren't going to the hotel, but it doesn't know that. I need to change it for the local airport."

The GPS system speaks up again. "You have missed your turn. Please turn left at the next intersection."

"Are you gonna take that from that bitch?" Stanley asks.

"Are you serious?"

"I don't care for her tone John, that's all, but if you like being dominated and bossed around by a woman that's your business."

"It's a machine Stanley, not a woman. Your issues with them not withstanding, it is a recording of a voice."

"I'm only saying…"

"You're always only saying something, so how about shutting up for a minute?"

The GPS pipes in again. "Turn left in 500 feet."

"She couldn't say 'please turn left' or add sweetie or baby to it?"

John purses his lips, furrows his eyebrows, and takes a deep breath before saying, "I know you're bored, but you need to take up another cross to bear, okay? You're starting to bug the shit out of me. We just found out the government is involved. Stanley, be serious for a change will you."

"Maybe involved," Stanley corrects him.

"Okay, maybe involved," John agrees.

Stanley starts analyzing the situation. "And one car with government tags does not mean the government is involved John, jeesh…"

"Okay, live in denial if you like but I know we have pissed off someone."

"You are always pissing off someone John. I just meant it doesn't mean it's caught the attention of the President of the United States yet."

"Shut up."

"Oh my, you suddenly have a spine but you let this bitch here boss you around. I see how it is John," Stanley says while gesturing to the GPS unit in the car.

"Recalculating…" says the GPS voice.

"You see? She admits it! I wish they would all admit they are always 'recalculating' and 'calculating' some shit on our ass."

"Are you off your meds today?" John asks. "Just imagine it's a young babe talking to you. What's the harm in that?"

"Oh you'd like to think that wouldn't you?" Stanley retorts. "It's the hot ones that are the most manipulative you know John."

"Oh! Another lesson from your playbook 'Men are from Mars and Think with Their Penis'?"

"Cute, but not a bad title come to think of it."

"I'll take your word for it." Pretending to be writing a book, John continues, "The hot ones are more manipulative. Got it."

"You should thank me. It's experience talking, believe me."

"Oh I believe that part. I really do."

After a few more quick turns to be sure no one is following them, John drives the Cadillac straight to the airport.

"We're almost at the airport John," Stanley says surprised.

"Where did you think I was going?"

"Back to the hotel."

"Are you dumb as well as blind? We went over this already."

"Okay, but I thought when we lost them; we would go to the hotel."

"I'm sure they know where we are staying Stanley."

"I'm going to have to buy all new toiletries and some more clothes John. Damn, even more money down the tubes and we are not making any money yet in all of this. I am not a happy camper John."

"I know you're not, but what about the time we spent money and time chasing that stewardess for you?"

"Airline personnel. I think they dislike Stewardess these days. Okay, okay, I'll go to Paris with you John, but I only have seven more days I can miss on my vacation time and I feel like I'm wasting it."

"Then go back to work. I'll be fine."

Stanley has to fight back hysterical laughter when he looks at John. "First, I'd never hear the end of it if I took you up on that little offer. Second, I doubt you have the courage to fly anywhere alone, let alone Paris. And third, if I am going to waste time, I would imagine that it would be wasted much nicer in Paris than here."

CHAPTER EIGHT

At the airport, John parks the Cadillac in Long Term Parking, not knowing if or when they may need it again, and the two of them proceed into the terminal to buy their tickets. After getting their tickets, during which time Stanley lectures John on the high cost because they were buying them at the last minute, the duo head for the one of the airport lounges before making their way through the security checkpoint. Stanley orders a Cosmopolitan and John goes for a shot of Captain and Coke.

"Oh, that reminds me," Stanley says, reaching into his pocket and pulling out a small white pill. "You should be falling on your knees with gratitude that I just happened to have one with me. Of course if we had stopped at the hotel like normal people, I'd have my toiletry bag and full prescription bottle, but nooo, you have to throw reason to the wind and come straight here."

"Just shut up already and give me the damn pill!"

Stanley drops the pill into John's hand. He washes it down with a swig of Captain and Coke, much to Stanley's dismay. "John, I don't think drinking is smart if you're going to take Xanax."

"Look," John explains, "you love to fly but I don't, and if I pass out, so be it. Trust me it's better for you anyway."

"Okay, but I don't want you acting all weird on me like the time you had your wisdom teeth out and took too many percodin tablets. People pay for that kind of feeling, you know John, and you just wasted it."

"Wasted it?"

"Wasted it John. You are the only person I know that can take a pain pill and muscle relaxant and end up having an anxiety attack."

"You mean I'm special?" John asks smiling.

"No, you're a control freak, which is probably why you hate flying."

"Well Dr. Joyce Brothers, as much as I do appreciate your psychological estimate me, everyone has their idiosyncrasies."

"Another word I haven't heard since college. Thank you for that blast from the past, and I don't have any weird idiosyncrasies like yours."

"Oh no?"

"No."

"How about how much you fidget with your balls?"

"What do you mean by that?"

"You must realize you fidget a lot down there."

"What?"

"Play with yourself a lot."

"Are you trying to ask me a question?"

"No...I'm pointing out that you touch your crotch a lot."

"Define 'a lot'," Stanley says indignantly.

"Too damn much, okay?"

"You're the crotch police now?"

"No, I don't have to be. You do it too damn much by anyone's standards, other than maybe a forward on the Lakers, which you are not."

"That's gross, and stereotypical, by the way."

"You bet it's gross! I don't think I've ever seen you wash your hands."

"You're just trying to be bitchy to get me back for…"

"It's a habit with you. Maybe you don't realize how much you do it but it's embarrassing, is what it is. You were just doing it again. I know you're bored in all of this, but we may be onto something historically important."

"Embarrassing for whom?"

"It should be for you, but it is for me to have to watch it."

"Women dig it."

"What?" John asks incredulously. "Women dig seeing you adjusting your crotch?"

"Yes."

"And one told you this?"

"You pick your nose," Stanley says, trying to deflect the criticism.

"Okay, so here we go. Trying to make things even, it's a competition now."

"You do."

"I do not."

"You pick your nose more than I play with my crotch."

"If I had all the snot in China, that wouldn't be true."

"Well, if it's that damn upsetting for you!"

"It is."

"Then I'll try and slow my roll."

John turns and looks at Stanley with a mixture of curious wonder and absolute disgust. "My God, slow your what?"

"My roll," Stanley says matter of factly.

"Now you even talk like a Laker."

"Just because you are stunningly un-hip, don't be a hater John."

"So now it's hip to fidget with your crotch?"

"I don't do it on purpose, per se. I scratch because they are there John."

"No, you scratch because they have been everywhere Stan."

"Jealous?"

"Of an STD? Hardly!"

"To be honest, I don't really realize I'm doing it."

"So that makes it okay?" John asks.

"No."

"I was just making you aware of it."

"You know what I'm aware of now?" Stanley asks.

"What?"

"How much you stare at my crotch! Before I had no idea…"

"Don't be such a narcissist."

"You know you might enjoy a tug or pull or scratch yourself every now and then. Loosen things up a bit."

"So you do know you're doing it, and you do it for pleasure. Is that what you're telling me now?"

"Do you hear how uptight you are John? You probably should have a drink after all." Stanley tells him with an edge of insulted and snideness in his tone.

"All I wanted was for you to see that you handle your balls like a Laker."

"John, a sports metaphor coming from you is like an exercise tip from a fat kid."

"I was trying to be a friend, that's all, and make you aware of a nasty habit you yourself said you weren't aware of. By the way, at the risk of continuing this stupid conversation, why in the world you would think a woman would like seeing you do that?"

"Not like it, but it makes them look, you know, and think, you know…"

"Think what? That you have Crabs?"

"No… Sexy thoughts about getting it on."

"Have you been listening to that 70s radio station again?" John shifts in his chair to face Stanley. "Let me get this straight. You think you need to point out to a possible admirer that you in fact, have a dick?"

"It's better than being one John."

"Well obviously this is, should you excuse my phrase, a touchy subject so let's drop it."

"Fine by me," Stanley says. "Just get in line. They've called our boarding section twice already."

The plane is a wide bodied jet with three rows of seats and two aisles. That would be comforting to many reluctant flyers, but not John. The two sit in their assigned seats on the left side of the plane with John by the window. Once seated, he promptly draws down the shade on the window so he can't see out.

Stanley gets a soda and rents a pair of headphones. After takeoff he wastes no time in watching the in-flight opening advertisements and movie. "Jesus John!" Stanley says, far too loudly, as he is wearing the headphones.

"Shhh…" John says, pulling one of his ear buds out of his head.

"Hey! Why'd you do that?" Stanley barks at him.

"You're yelling idiot. What's wrong anyway? Am I not nerve wracked enough for you on this flight? Actually, I am even more nervous than usual for me. Stanley how do you stay so calm in all this turbulence?"

"This is not turbulence per se, just some air pockets."

"Can't they fly smoother?" John pleads.

"We've been through all this before John. It is a smooth flight as far as these things go. We are above the ocean for God's sake."

"Did you have to remind me of that? I thought you yelled Jesus to tell me something. Maybe something that would take my mind off of the flight."

"No, I yelled Jesus because that last bump hurt me too…"

"But you love to fly."

"Yeah, I mean my butt. I had a tough bowel movement back at Mrs. Birch's place that I think tore my asshole a little bit."

"Stanley…"

"Yes John?"

"I'm not Oprah. Don't feel like you have to tell me everything, okay?"

116

"I'm sorry if the image was too much for you, you sissy."

"That, coupled with the fact I know for a fact that you didn't wash your hands before we ate in the airport."

"So?"

"So…you have now informed me that you had your finger in your ass."

"I never said that."

"You said you thought there was a tear in your asshole."

"Yeah. So?"

"How would you know you had a tear unless…"

"Okay, okay. Let's say for a minute I had my finger in there, purely exploratory by the way, not a kinky thing."

"My point is you ate after that without washing your hands. Correct?"

"What are you, my mother now? I happen to know you didn't wash your hands before you ate either John," Stanley says defiantly.

"Ah, but I didn't have my finger in my ass."

"Yes, and if I had had my finger in your ass, I would've washed my hands, but I didn't. I had it in my ass."

"So your ass is cleaner than my ass. Is that what you're saying to me?"

"No, well yes, probably, but no, I mean it's my ass, so it's all good, you know?"

"You're sick," John says, disgusted with the conversation.

"Am I? Or am just I being honest?" Stanley asks.

""What? No you are just sick."

"Look," Stanley says, trying to prove his point, "have you ever dropped a piece of food you were cooking on the floor and picked it up, dusted it off, and still ate it?"

"Yes, but I don't see…"

"Uhhh listen. But what if I dropped a piece of your food on the ground, dusted it off, and offered it for you to eat. Would you eat it?

"No, of course not."

"Exactly!" Stanley exclaims triumphantly.

"Exactly what? You can't just say exactly Stanley. People say exactly Stanley when they make a point."

"Exactly."

"Let's change the subject to something a little less nauseating," John says.

"Fine by me." Stanley glances back up at the monitor showing an assortment of ads before getting to the in-flight movie. "Hey John…They have in-flight advertising for Christ's sake."

"So?"

"So? That's tacky John, and as you know, I am all for making a buck, but really John, advertising to us here so high up and all? That's not Kosher."

"We are a captive audience Stanley."

"That doesn't make it right."

"What's so offensive to you about a couple of ads?" John asks, not really wanting to know the answer.

"The ads are for medical crap and symptoms and conditions. Have you ever noticed how much of that there is on TV these days?"

"So?"

"So, it's depressing, that's so. They are peddling a pill for this and that disease and ailments that I have never heard of."

Realizing he's right, John says, "Well, come to think of it, there are more commercials like that these days."

"Exactly, and the pharmaceutical companies are who's behind it all."

"Well as much as I love a good conspiracy as you know Stanley, that's just stupid. The answer is actually fairly simple."

"Which is?" Stanley asks impatiently.

"Baby boomers. They are all getting older. The first boomers have already hit 60 and the population is older than ever before in large numbers, so the ads just reflect where the money's being spent; on quality of life stuff."

"Quality of life? Well, they've sold you I see. There's no quality of life in electronic wheelchairs and disposable diapers for adults John. Those bastards at the pharmaceutical companies are still not innocent in my book."

"What's with you and pharmaceutical companies?" John asks.

"I just don't trust them, that's all."

"Well, God forbid you should ever need a drug for something serious one day. I'll bet then you'll be singing another tune."

"Don't be so sure. I mean, I get what you're saying. Sure, I'm no fool. I'd take the damn pill and be happy I'm alive and all."

"Exactly my point."

"But, and here's the rub John, it may cure whatever ails me, but then I'll end up with lactating breasts or something like that."

"Lactating breasts? I don't think that's possible Stanley. You are a male you know."

"I know, but we also have female hormones too John."

"Estrogen, you mean?"

"Yes, estrogen. You see, you did know!"

"You've been reading again haven't you Stanley? How many times have I warned you about that?"

"Cute John, cute. You're saying we don't have estrogen in our bodies cause we're men?"

"No, I'm saying we don't have breast milk in our bodies because we're men."

"No, not now. Not until you take some new drug, then bam…squirt, squirt."

"I give up."

"What you mean to say is I won this little argument," Stanley says triumphantly.

"No, I mean I give up. I am at a loss at how to explain to you the utter impossibility of your man boobs leaking anything, much less milk."

"I knew it. I won."

"If that makes you feel better, that's fine."

"Here's a thought for you John. What would happen if you took one of these drugs and it made your breasts leak milk, but and here's the tricky part, you were lactose intolerant? Huh? Then what smart guy?"

Playing into Stanley's paranoid thinking, John says, "Those devious bastards! I see why you don't trust them now."

"You're being sarcastic I get it, but what would happen?"

"I suppose you would have an allergic reaction to your own body Stanley."

"Sinister…"

"Stanley, my God. I'm only kidding."

"I wouldn't put it past those people." Stanley says indignantly.

"What people?"

"The pharmaceutical people John, are you even listening to me? I'm trying to warn and educate you."

"Well warn me on the ground. I'm not in the mood for your warnings at 10,000 feet."

"Oh we're much higher than 10,000 feet, which is why if the cabin depressurized, those little oxygen masks would fall down unless you were unconscious by then, in which case…"

"You win."

"I win what?" Stanley asks.

"Let's talk about mens lactating breasts."

"What changed your mind?"

"I'd rather listen to you talk about something that absurd than real statistics on flying disasters."

"Oh, sorry about that chief. Look, if it makes you feel better I've never been on a flight where the oxygen masks fell down."

"Swell. Very comforting."

"I mean not because they malfunctioned, but because they didn't need to fall down."

"Could you change the damn subject already?" John asks noticeably irritated.

"Okay, okay, sorry. Mea culpa." Changing subjects, Stanley asks, "Did you see the cute red-head who served me my drink?"

"Yes."

"You don't sound impressed."

"I don't like red-heads the way you do, you know that."

"That's really a narrow way of thinking John."

"I think I will be fine picking from brunettes, black-haired, and blonde women. I don't think I've narrowed my field that much. Besides, it's been my experience that most red-heads I've known were nuts."

"You think all red-heads are nuts but then you don't respect my opinion of pharmaceutical companies?"

"Just go back to listening to your movie. The commercials, you'll be happy to know, have all ended."

"Okay, okay, if you need me, just tap me on the shoulder."

"Okay, 'Mr. Helpful' I'll do that."

"No need to be snotty just because you're tense." Stanley says, putting the ear plug back in his ear.

John lies back on his pillow. He shuts his eyes and tries to think of anything other than falling oxygen masks and lactating male breasts.

After a few minutes, Stanley pulls out an ear plug and starts talking to John. "Why are you so scared of plane travel anyway John?"

"I don't want to die alone."

"But you wouldn't. You'd go out with a few hundred other terrified people," Stanley says grinning.

"That's not my idea of a great finish either Stanley."

"Oh, now you're just being picky, that's all."

John opens his eyes and sits up a little. "You mean you would really want to die on a plane full of people?"

"Well, no, but I certainly wouldn't take it personally or feel singled out if I did now. How could I?"

"You do have an interesting way of looking at things Stanley. I'll give you that much. Twisted, but interesting."

"Thank you John. I will take that as a compliment."

"I was sure that you would."

"Life is very yin and yang you know John."

"Are you getting philosophical on me now Stanley?"

"I'm deeper than I look."

"You'd almost have to be," John says.

"I'm serious here," Stanley insists.

"For a change…" John teases.

"Yes, for a change."

Rolling his eyes while giving in, John says, "Okay, okay. Give me an example of yin and yang Stanley. Maybe it will keep my mind off of this flight."

"Okay. A woman goes to the gym to work out and look hot and get a slammin' body. You with me so far?"

"Sadly yes."

"However you get on board is fine with me," Stanley says as he continues. "Now the woman works out hard to get a nice, tight ass."

"Stanley…"

"Listen, I'm being serious, remember?"

"Okay, go on."

"The kind on ass you could bounce a quarter off of. But, while she's there getting leaner and more muscular in the pursuit of the great ass, she is also losing fat."

"Naturally," John interjects.

"Right, which is a good thing. Right?"

"Yes it is, I suppose." John is still feigning interest to take his mind off the bumpy flight.

"Normally you would be correct John, but the problem is the boobs."

"The boobs?" John asks quizzically.

"Yes. Boobs are made of fat," Stanley says with authority. "I think like 89% in fact."

"Is that an actual statistic Stanley?"

"Yes."

"You've researched this I see." John says sarcastically.

"Yes I have," Stanley says defensively. "So you see where I'm going with all of this?"

"Thankfully, no, I do not."

"Her ass looks better, but her boobs suffer in the process. She loses inches yes, but also in the rack, which most definitely is not good." Stanley explains. "Yin and yang give and take John."

"Cause and effect," John says.

"What?"

"Nothing, just trying to stay interested Stanley. Did you have help with that theory?"

"Of course not."

"Of course is what I was thinking."

"It's all true John. Look it up."

"You should really ask questions about things you don't understand when you're reading something Stanley."

A short dinging sound indicates the pilot has made an adjustment. "Good news John. The signs say we can unbuckle and move around the cabin." Stanley asks, changing the subject.

"You unbuckle and move around. I'm staying put."

"Do what you want. I thought I saw a cute stewardess in the back that doesn't serve our row." Stanley giggles a little and says, "Not yet anyway. Maybe I can talk her into putting in for a transfer."

"Trying to add to your 'mile high club' experiences Stanley?"

"That would be nice, wouldn't it? But probably not."

"Negative Stanley? And about a woman no less! What's wrong with this picture?" John asks.

"Realistic, but never negative," Stanley reassures him while starting to stand up. Before he can, John moves his upright tray down, startling Stanley in the process and causing him to jump.

John looks up at him and asks, "Were you beat as a child Stanley? Why do you flinch so easily?"

"Yes, repeatedly, sometimes by complete strangers. I don't want to talk about it. To this day, I flinch if somebody tries to hold a door open for me."

"Okay then," John says rolling his eyes.

Stanley looks up at the video monitors and then at John. "I'm not sure how appropriate it is showing the film 'Castaway' as the in-flight film John. I think I'm going to go make friends and not watch it after all."

"Whatever…"

"It's probably a good idea you miss it too John."

"Why? It stars Tom Hanks doesn't it? I like Tom Hanks."

"Yes, and there's a plane crash in the opening and he's stranded on a desert island throughout the movie."

"What the hell were they thinking showing that?" John asks agitated.

"That's what I thought, but I guess the whole survivor plot line is the upbeat part."

"That he survives?"

"Yes, under incredible odds, blah, blah, blah… You know who the ultimate survivor is to me John?"

"I can't even imagine. Tom Hanks?"

"No. Paul is the ultimate survivor, now isn't he?"

"Paul who?"

"McCartney."

"The Beatle?"

"Yes," Stanley answers.

"I dare to ask but, how is he the ultimate survivor?" John asks with sarcasm in his voice.

"He's the last Beatle standing isn't he?"

"Uhm, if by standing you mean alive, then you're a little off, as usual."

"How so? He was a Beatle wasn't he?"

"Yes, but I believe Ringo Starr is also still alive."

"You sure about that?"

"Well I haven't spoken to him today, but fairly sure, yes."

"Well that Ringo was always surprising people," Stanley says almost to himself.

"Well I try and live by the immortal words of Paul, who wrote and I think I quote here; 'When you were young and your heart was an open book, you used to say live and let live. But if this ever-changing world in which we live in make you give in and sigh, I say live and let die."

John shoots Stanley the most sarcastically amused look during the entire trip so far. "Apostle Paul said that, did he?"

"No, I said immortal Paul, not apostle Paul. I never said he was an apostle so there's no reason for sarcasm 'Saint John'."

"Reading from the book of Paul I suppose Stanley?" John asks smiling.

"Make fun all you want John. You have your Bible and I have mine." When John starts laughing, Stanley changes the subject. "Which one would you have done – made – had sex with?"

The laughter turns to a cough. "Excuse me? Please God; tell me we aren't still talking about The Beatles." He looks at Stanley with a very serious expression. "They are all men for God's sake, and I'm straight."

"Well sure you are. So am I, but you have an opinion on the subject don't you?"

Realizing he's serious, John says, "Actually no. It has never come up as strange as you may find that to be. Two are dead, by the way, which cranks up the strangeness factor on this a bit higher than your normal polls you've given me in the past."

"When they were young, not now. I thought I'd made that detail clear before, sorry." Stanley says. "Ed Sullivan young okay. Who would you have done?"

"Seriously, are you waiting on an answer to this?" John asks incredulously.

"Seriously." Stanley states.

"Seriously, I'd probably have done Ed."

Stanley gives John a shocked look. "Come on, that's not being serious. Besides, Ed had a face like a mule!"

"Be serious? How can I take a conversation about which Beatle I'd have sex with seriously? Besides, Ed could have helped my career." John adds sarcastically.

"John was killed by a stalker."

"Yes I know, very sad."

"Women threw panties on the stage at Paul all the time though. He's the only real choice don't you think?" Stanley asks.

"I think you have an issue or two, or three, or four to deal with. That's what I think…"

"He's the only Beatle that was good looking, that's really the point I'm trying to make." Stanley says.

"Looks are very subjective Stanley. Some people may not agree with you. Some people think Barbra Streisand is a great beauty and some…"

"And some," Stanley interrupts, "wear glasses to correct their vision."

"See, that's exactly my point. Everyone doesn't agree on what's beautiful."

"So you think there are people – male people – straight male people over the age of say, six, who look at Pamela Anderson and go, uh, not really my type."

"Yes, I really do."

"Perhaps you run in a different crowd than I do." Stanley says.

"I run in your crowd with you, moron."

"Well, I'm just trying to keep it real, that's all. So, who would you have done?" Stanley asks again. "Come on, it's Paul. Am I right, it's Paul?"

"I'm not answering this stupid premise."

"Admit it."

"No, I'm not admitting anything."

"Admit it. Come on." Stanley pressures.

Finally exasperated, John says, "Alright! Paul."

"I knew it! It had to be Paul. He was the only sane choice really."

"What sanity had to do with that line of questioning is beyond me." The lights in the plane's cabin start to go down. "The lights are being turned off in the cabin Stanley. What's wrong?" John asks while becoming anxious.

"Quit panicking John. It's late at night and people want to sleep. You want a pillow?"

John shakes his head. "No, I've got one thanks."

"You gonna be okay Johnny?" Stanley asks, noting that John was getting anxious."

"Yes, the Xanax always makes me sleepy. I'll be fine."

"Get some sleep," Stanley says.

"You too," John replies as he clicks up his tray and then turns towards the window.

Hours later, John wakes to see sunshine streaming through the cabin of the plane. Rubbing his eyes, he turns to Stanley, who is listening to a CD player and nudges him. "Where are we?"

Stanley looks at his friend and jokingly says, "On a plane bound for Paris."

"Really? I could have figured that much out." John sneers at him.

""You wanted something more specific?" Stanley asks sarcastically.

"Yes please."

"I'm not the pilot John. How am I supposed to know exactly where we are?" As Stanley says the last few words, the fasten seat belts light came on. He looks up at the light and then back to John. "I think we are preparing to land John."

"Great," John says sarcastically. "I had to wake up now."

"You prefer the alternative?"

"No, it's just that I had hoped I'd have more time awake to think over our game plan, but I slept most of the trip away."

"We were beat and you were under the influence of narcotics. Besides, when do you ever have a 'game plan' as you put it?"

"Why not say that a little louder, or better yet, when we're going through Customs." John barks at Stanley. "And I do have a plan. The plan is to do some press when we land."

"Do some press... how so?" Stanley asks.

"When we land, let's call your company's publicity office, and see if we can leak some information to the press like I told you before about why we're here."

"Why are we here John? Let's start with me finding out."

"To look at the clues we have uncovered in all of this mess so far. His apartment, his grave, and things like that. I want it leaked to the press that we are authors in search of truths to write about Morrison's final days here in Paris."

"Okay, I'll see who I can con for you, but what do you think will happen then? Seriously John."

"I don't know," John says, shrugging his shoulders.

Stanley shifts in his chair. "Okay, buckle up John, we are landing."

John looks at Stanley. "I'm still buckled up. I never removed the buckle."

"Of course you are. Of course you are John." Stanley says patting him on the top of the head condescendingly.

"You know Stanley; you always say I'm the only one freaked out about flying, so, then why is it always so quiet you could hear a pin drop whenever a plane is landing?" John asks.

"Well, you may have a point there."

The landing was smooth, soothing John a bit, and the plane quickly taxies up to the building as the airport's personnel attach the moving hallway to the plane's fuselage. Getting up from their seats, Stanley looks at John and says, "Let's get our bags."

"What bags?" John asks.

"Oh yeah, right. Sorry, just a habit. Then let's get a car and find a nice hotel. I'd like a nap. I didn't sleep as much as you did."

The two exit the plane and walk outside to the front of the terminal to hail a cab and settle into the back seat of the first one that stops for them.

"Please take us to the Ritz Carlton on the Champ De Ellyses."

"Pardon moi?" The driver asks.

"The Ritz Carlton." Stanley says again.

"Le Quelle?" The driver asks again.

Getting quickly frustrated, Stanley asks John, "What the hell is Frenchie saying John?"

"He asked you which Ritz Carlton in French, HIS native tongue."

"That's great for him, but I don't know French," Stanley replies.

"Qua?" The cab driver asks one more time.

John looks at Stanley. "He still needs an answer Stanley. Don't be the ugly American please."

"Are you kidding me? Hey pal, you picked us up at American Airlines! American, get it?"

"Oh God, here we go..." John says.

The driver speaks again saying, "Vata ser uncul sal American" and spits.

"Oh, he gets it alright Stanley." John proceeds to translate the driver's last comment to Stanley. "He said 'go fuck yourself you filthy American'." Looking at Stanley's disgusted expression, John continues. "Okay, so you are the stereotypical, ugly American. Great!"

"What? Did he call me ugly John?"

John shakes his head in disbelief at Stanley's ignorance before leaning up to the driver's seat and in perfect French says, "Sir, please take us to the Ritz Hotel at 1188 Champs-Élysées."

"Yeah, I think it best you talk to him," Stanley says in a huff, crossing his arms at his chest.

"I agree," John says, shooting Stanley a dirty look. "I know how mad you get at home when you call someplace and it asks you to press one for English Stanley, but…"

"You're damned right that ticks me off, and it should you too!"

"Why? I remember in a college class once being taught that our country narrowly missed by only a vote or two of adopting German as its national language. Did you know that Stanley?"

"Yes, I believe that's true. So then, how is it two hundred plus years later, they tell us we never voted on a national language, and now we need to?"

"I don't actually know how to answer that, come to think of it." John says.

"Aha!" Stanley exclaims triumphantly.

"Aha?"

"It's not often I ever hear you say something like that."

"Like what?"

"That you don't have an answer."

"Let's just say it's not high on my priority list."

"You aren't fit to be an American!" Stanley says in a huff, re-folding his arms as the cab driver pulls up to their chosen hotel.

CHAPTER NINE

Walking into the Ritz, they immediately notice the beauty and grandeur of the place. So accustomed to traveling in the States at cookie cutter places like the Hilton and Marriott, this building is probably 200-years-old with elegant staircases, crystal chandeliers in the lobby providing lighting for the Persian rugs covering the marble floors. It's very beautiful in all.

They cross to the solid mahogany counter where a bellman asks if they have any luggage, and then gives them an odd look when John replies that they don't. They're quickly checked in by a woman behind the counter.

Once in their rooms, Stanley calls his banking contacts in the press department to arrange for a press conference the next morning. It's not long before they begin hearing from members of the media.

"Hey John," Stanley says. "The local news bureau called and said they would come around to the hotel in the morning at approximately 9:00am."

"Great, then for tonight, let's just relax and enjoy some famous Parisian cooking and start early in the morning with the press conference." John says as he eases into a chair.

Stanley looks at him. "What are you going to say exactly at the conference pray tell?"

"That we are two American journalists who were hired to write a fresh, newsy book on the death of Jim Morrison; hence our arrival in Paris, and that, unlike past books, ours promises some shocking new evidence concerning his death..."

Stanley seems a bit confused as he says, "But we don't have shocking new evidence concerning his death. We don't even have shocking old evidence."

"That's true, but the press doesn't know that. They will lap it up and every crackpot in the world will contact us eventually with their theories."

"And that's a good thing?" Stanley asks.

"No, that's bad, but hopefully we will also illicit interest from our tail in the U.S."

"Do you really think that whoever followed us twice over there would follow us here to Paris?" Stanley asks.

"Maybe. Maybe not." John answers matter-of-factly.

"If it's merely some lackey working for the overzealous owner of those letters, I think not." Stanley says.

"Believe it or not, I agree with you if that is the correct assumption, but if they have more at stake or more to hide than just those letters, they may already be in Paris." John says more somberly now, not knowing just how right he was. "Come on. Let's eat something."

"No, you go ahead. Like I said before, I want to sleep."

"Okay, but you're missing out on some great food here." John says, trying to tempt him.

"Do they have a Chick-fil-A?" Stanley asks.

"I doubt it Stanley."

"Five Guys burgers then?"

"No."

"Then I'm not missing out on anything except sleep." Stanley says as he stretches out on the bed.

"Suit yourself," John says. "I'll be next door in my suite if you need me after I get back from dinner." He turns to leave and then turns back to Stanley. "My cell phone isn't working yet. I need to call and tell them where I am."

"Whatever. I'll be fine 'Mom'. Just let me sleep. Get me up in the morning in time for me to shower before the press conference. Okay? Goodnight."

"Nitey, nite Stanley." John says condescendingly. He heads downstairs and eats in the restaurant before returning to his room a short time later.

Lying in bed, John tries to organize his thoughts on what he would say in the morning, wondering how many people would show up, and all of the logistics that fill his head as he drifts off to sleep with the biggest question of all; how many press people will show up?

He and Stanley, as it turns out, are actually surprised at the turnout of the local press for their conference the next morning. They expected the main news bureau as promised, but six other news services showed up as well. John speaks briefly, covering the ground he had agreed on earlier with Stanley before taking questions from the press.

"Monsieur Black, it is now held in widespread belief after the old employees of the nightclub 'Rock and Roll Circus' came forward last year, last Jim Morrison actually died of a heroin overdose in their club, and his own drug connection took him back to his apartment to be found by the emergency responders later," a French journalist states.

"Well," John authoritively replies, "we have concrete proof that may make that just another in a long line of Morrison folktales and fabrications."

"Is there anything you can share with us now?" asks another man from another news agency.

"Only that we now believe Jim Morrison may have met with foul play in this beautiful city and a cover-up obscured the real cause of his death for all of these years." John says.

"Then you do believe he is dead?" asks one of the journalists while the room full start to snicker and make quiet comments.

John quells their comments by stating, "Yes, we are not supporters of the 'Jim is alive' theory." He smiles and uses air quotes. "We are only here to suggest and to likely prove for the first time in history," John says adding dramatic tone to his remaining words, "that his death may have not been an accidental overdose or an overdose of any kind."

"So you intend to prove it was murder?" asks a journalist trying to gain more information for his paper and a better, more spectacular quote.

"You will have to wait on the book," John says diplomatically while smiling to the crowd. "We only wanted to give respect to the local Parisian press and let them know our research has brought us to their beautiful city of lights."

The press members and those gathered applaude as John and Stanley head across the lobby to an elevator.

Once inside, Stanley looks at John. "I can't believe they even applauded in the end for you."

"Jealous?" John asks, smiling at his performance.

"No, it's just that you were like a politician in that you didn't tell them anything. Besides, Morrison was an American so why do they give a damn?"

"Because his grave is a big tourist attraction here, and they have become associated with his legend as much as we are in the States."

"So they are thrilled that he died in their little city basically?"

"Something like that, yes." John begins to fidget in his suit jacket and sees wrinkles in the elevator's mirrors. "We need to go buy some clothes Stanley. I don't know about you, but my outfit is getting ripe," he says, tugging at his collar.

"Goodwill?" Stanley asks back. "Salvation Army perhaps?"

"It was a rhetorical question that did not require an answer from you."

"I know what rhetorical means. I was trying to educate you John. All the expensive crap you buy ends up at Goodwill for pennies on the dollar. Clothes, especially couture and the like are not a good investment."

"When I want your investment advice I will ask for it. In the meantime 'Uncle Scrooge', try to relax and enjoy. Besides, you're a frickin' fashion plate compared to me," John says.

"Yes, and I buy them all at thrift stores, outlet centers…"

"I get it, I get it."

As the door swings open into John's room, it looks like a tornado has ripped through the place. "And you call me a pig," Stanley says.

"You are a pig. My room's been tossed you idiot."

"Tossed?" Stanley asks.

"Searched."

"I know what it means," Stanley smirks, "I just couldn't believe you said tossed." He walks to the adjoining door and swings it open. "Great. Mine too," he says, looking into his room and seeing it destroyed.

Looking through the door, John smirks and asks, "How can you tell?"

"You're a riot John. How many times have you been divorced again? I don't understand those foolish women's choices." Stanley says ever-so-snidely.

"Well, we were followed, that's for sure," John says, ignoring Stanley's dig.

"Or maybe they called friends in Paris." Stanley becomes more sarcastic. "Great, we have no extra clothes and no, what's the word I'm thinking of? Oh yeah, no gun!"

"No one's shot at us. We don't need a gun. They just want to know what we know so far," John says "hopefully."

"Yes, so far," Stanley repeats. "Which is nothing, by the way."

"True, but they don't know that."

"I wish they did. So we have made ourselves targets and when the bad guys catch up to us and tell they are going to make us talk, we won't even have anything to tell them, which they won't believe and then..."

"You watch too much television Stanley."

"Do you really still think it was prudent to say in the press conference that we are looking for help in our research from anyone who knows of the events in Morrison's Paris time?"

"Yes, I do," John says. "We needed to do that for several reasons. One, we may get someone who really knows something new. Wouldn't that be a kick?"

"And number two?" Stanley prods.

"And second, it opens the door for the people following us to contact us as well."

"I was afraid you'd say that, but did you also have to offer money for new information? Haven't we lost enough for you already?"

John looks at Stanley and tries to snow him. "We are a profit-making pair of authors who are writing a book with a sensational hook, in which case, if that were true, we would be offering money if it helped our book. Get it? It's all part of the appearance."

"You have not forgotten all of that was a bull shit cover story then?" Stanley asks.

"No I haven't," John says tersely.

"Good, I was worried for a minute there that you believe your own press release. Now what?" Stanley asks.

"Clean up our rooms maybe." John suggests.

"Report it you meant to say, don't you?"

"No."

"Why not?" Stanley demands.

"That would tell other people we may have something worth taking. No, we know, and the people who did it know, and that's all that needs to be in the loop for now."

"You said the press conference would protect us Johnny, not make us a living pair of targets."

"Yes, by going public no one would dare harm us." John says.

"You believe that do you?" Stanley asks him.

"Yes I do," John says.

"Okay. I will cling to that naïve belief of yours," Stanley says. "Can we go clothes shopping now? I think I've pissed my only good pants and need more."

"There you go again Oprah. Too much damn information again."

"You know calling me Oprah is not the insult you think it is."

"Oh, now you wish you were Oprah?"

"No shit! She is loaded and powerful, that one is. I bet she knows what happened to Morrison."

"I doubt it."

"And Kennedy, and at Roswell."

"I doubt it. She is rich and powerful though, I'll give you that much."

"Oh shit!" Stanley says suddenly.

"What now?" John asks.

"Look at that!" Stanley says, pointing to the mirror above his chest of drawers. On it are the words written in what appears to be marker that say, 'Stop while you can.' Stanley takes a step backwards. "Well, that's it for me," he says. "It seems fairly self-explanatory, don't you think?"

"Maybe it's from one of your conquests." John says, trying to make light of the situation. "How do I know what you did last night?"

"I slept, that's what I did asshole."

"Maybe you wrote it."

"Are you frickin' serious? It's not my handwriting for starters John. Seriously!"

"Okay, okay, so they want to frighten us," John says.

"Bingo, we have a winner! It worked for me, how you feeling?" Stanley asks excitedly.

"It's just words on a mirror," John stresses.

"No, it's an ominous warning left for us!" Stanley says, gesturing back and forth between them with his hand.

"Come on, nothing's changed. Just clean the mirror before the maids see it."

"What about the cops seeing it?" Stanley asks.

"No. I told you no, and I told you why!" John barks.

CHAPTER TEN

After rearranging their rooms and going downstairs to an assortment of boutiques for clothes, John and Stanley meet again in the lobby's dining room and sit down to eat. John has a rather large stack of notes in his hand.

"Hey Stanley, I already have some messages and leads. The news organizations' stories on our press conference are only just now hitting!"

"Some messages?" Stanley asks looking incredulously at the stack of small pages in John's hand.

"Okay, a few more than that."

"A few? Please elaborate."

"Okay 42, but that's not the point."

"Sacrebleu! 42?"

"Brushing up on your French? Nice job Stanley." John mocks. "42 positive leads here in my hot little hand." He waves them in front of Stanley.

"You mean 42 nut cases." Stanley says.

"Okay, some seem a little weak." John admits.

"Like, for instance?"

"Well, one is a wican priest who says he has control of Jim Morrison's spirit and that we can interview him directly or uh, indirectly, I guess as the case may be."

"Well let's go with that one by all means. Cut out the middle man. I mean if Jim can't tell us about his letter writing back home, who can?" Stanley closes his eyes and shakes his head.

"I never said we wouldn't get some dubious leads Stanley."

"You call a wican priest a dubious lead? What the hell is a wican anyway?"

"A white witch I think. Something like that."

"So we've come to Paris for some 'Harry Potter' wannabe to tell us, directly from the horse's mouth no less, what happened? I'm worried about you."

"I didn't say we were making that particular appointment, but some do look promising. In fact, to be honest..."

"Oh God, I hate when you start a sentence that way." Stanley interrupted with a dirty look.

"I made us an appointment after dinner at a bar down the street from here."

"To see who?" Stanley asks.

"There is a man who left a message that he knows something about a letter Morrison sent the day before he died."

"A letter? Again with the letters..."

"Exactly why it seemed relevant to me. I'm glad you agree." John says sarcastically.

"Could be a set up Johnny."

"Well we are meeting in a nice, noisy bar. Outside no less, okay?"

"Okay, okay." Stanley drops his fork and pushes away his plate. "This food sucks."

John leans in and whispers, "Shh, don't let the chef hear you."

"The chef?" Stanley asks. "Oh I doubt seriously a chef was involved in this travesty. Or anyone else for that matter. I wish they had an In-N-Out Burger here. That one in Los Angeles was wonderful."

"Well they don't, so shut up."

"Thank God I found some Reese's Peanut Butter Cups in a store by the clothing boutique," Stanley says, taking a package out of his jacket pocket.

"So you want the chef to rifle our room next? Put that away, it's insulting!"

"It would also be insulting to have me passing out from a sugar crash at the table, don't you think?"

"Fine, just try to eat it surreptitiously."

"I see the word-a-day calendar is still working for you Johnny." Stanley says biting into the peanut butter cup. "Yeah," he says after a few chews, "that burger would've been better though. I even love the name – In-N-Out. Shit, now I'm hungry and horny."

"Well I can't help you with either one of those things, so keep it to yourself. Better still, just order a damn burger."

"Obviously you didn't notice there were no burgers on the menu Sherlock."

"Well I'm sure Room Service will make you one later, okay?"

"Okay, okay."

"The bar's within walking distance, let's go."

"How do you know the way?" Stanley asks surprised.

"I asked the concierge for directions."

"Please don't speak French to me. You know I don't like that."

"We say concierge anywhere we go Stanley."

"Oh yeah, right. Okay, I'm just a little sensitive after the taxi guy spit on me."

Walking out of the Ritz, John and Stanley begin the trek to the bar for their meeting. "It's pretty weather out tonight. At least there's no rain." John says while walking. "The bar's at the next corner and on the left."

"Did it occur to you the people following us might have been at the press conference John?"

"Yes, but so many people showed up I couldn't very well memorize them all. Why do you bring that up now?"

"Well, what if a competing newshound sets up an appointment with us just to pick our brains?"

"I had thought of that. We simply don't volunteer any information. We ask all the questions so it's one way communication only."

"And if they say something good you pay them how much? And whose money are we using pray tell?"

"I knew you'd get around to bringing that up eventually. Since this has been my lark, as you once put it, so fair is fair, I'll pay the green."

"Fair enough," Stanley says.

Walking into the Parisian bar, the two did as was agreed to earlier. John calls the man who wanted to meet them and sits down at an outside table by the street. After ordering drinks, Stanley pulls a cigar out of his jacket and starts to light up.

"Where did you get that thing and since when do you smoke?" John asks.

"Since I'm sitting in an outdoor bar in Paris no less, it seems only fitting. They sell them in the lobby if you must know." Stanley takes a puff. "Besides, this isn't Los Angeles. There seem to be a lot of smokers in Paris, doesn't there?"

"You think?" John asks sarcastically. "Just try not to blow that smelly crap at me alright?"

"I can't help where the wind blows things John."

A man suddenly appears at the side of the table. "Excuse me, Monsieur Black?"

"Yes," John says, rising halfway to shake hands with a man in his early to late sixties it would appear. "And this is my assistant, Mr. uh," he stammers.

"Dion," Stanley interrupts. "Steven Dion," he continues while John looked blankly at him.

"Yes, well you said you had information we may be able to use in our book and investigations?" John asks.

"Yes."

"About a letter I think you told me."

"Yes. My name is Gary Stand and I had a friend once in the publishing business in New York City by the name of Jonathan Dolger. He was, in fact, Jim Morrison's publishing contact. You may have run across his name in your research so far?"

"Go on," John says cryptically.

"The day before he died, Jim wrote a telegram to Dolger."

"About?" John asks.

"About changing the cover design on a book of poetry Jim was working on."

"Anything else?"

"Well I never saw the telegram, but as a fan of Morrison's, I asked him to see it. He told me for a while he thought some employee in the firm had it, so I began to pressure him to buy it. You know, as memorabilia."

"Yes. Go on."

"But then he said the truth was about a month after Morrison's death, a man contacted him and told him that he was with Jim when he died and would like to have the telegram. Dolger said he gave it to him but couldn't remember the man's name."

"That's odd, don't you think?" John asks.

"That's what I thought. Dolger's since passed away, but he never would tell me who asked for the telegram or why he gave it up like that."

"Anything else Mr. Stand?" John asks.

"No. I'm an American too but am visiting, saw your news blurb this morning and thought it would be fun to tell you this, and I kind of hoped it would make sense to you."

"Well sorry. No, it doesn't."

"I don't know the contents of the telegram. You can't use it in your book then," he says sounding disappointed.

"Not without more details no."

"I'm sorry."

"If it's money you want," John starts.

"No, no...I do well thanks. Just thought it would be fun, like I said, to look you up." He starts to get out of his chair. "Well, thanks for at least listening to me." He sticks out his hand to shake John's and Stanley's.

"No thank you for coming out tonight. We are staying at the Ritz Hotel in case you think of anything further that we may be able to use."

"Thanks. Goodnight Mr. Black, Mr. Dion," he says nodding at Stanley.

As he walks out onto the street, John turns to Stanley. "Mr. Dion?"

"Yeah, you know, like Celine Dion. She's French and I thought he'd think I was one of them."

"Until when, you spoke? Besides dumb ass, he was American and she is Canadian, not French."

"Then why does she speak French in interviews I have seen?"

"I am not up to explaining that to you right now. Besides, Dion reminds me more of the mustard."

"Fine," Stanley says. "Look, I'm bored again okay? Leave me alone. Although, I could also ask why you gave him our address for where we are, in fact, staying?"

"Why not? The bad guys already clearly know where we are staying."

"That's true. Unsettling, but true." Going back to the subject at hand, Stanley mocks, "Any more appointments 'Mr. Big Shot'?"

"I need to call more of them back and see if any sound promising." John stands up and motions for Stanley to do the same. "Let's go back to the hotel so I can use the room phone."

Walking back to their rooms in the hotel, John says, "Tomorrow, I want to go to the apartment he died in and the gravesite."

"Why?" Stanley asks. "What after all these years could you possibly hope to accomplish by doing that?"

"Why not you mean, don't you?"

"Ooh, you got me. It's hard to argue with logic like that."

"I looked at some internet articles on line from the French perspective on his death before I came to down to dinner."

"And?"

"And his personal physician, a Dr. Derum said he was in perfect health when he came to Paris, but most accounts say he packed on a lot of weight while here."

"The food and drinking," Stanley says. "Yes, that would do it."

"A heroin addict doesn't pack on weight though," John says.

"True."

"You know I also found out that Pamela Courson died only days before a judge was going to award her a fair share of the Morrison estate. A half million in cash and one-fourth interest in The Doors future earnings."

"Really? I didn't know that."

"Yes."

"That is strange. Seems she had lots to live for."

"Yes, as did Jim. I found out he told people often his parents were dead."

"Were they? I mean, Daddy was dead. I know Mom was alive."

"Not only were they both alive. His mother, as you know, died only a couple years ago and 'daddy' as you called him, was an Admiral in the Navy."

"Well that probably just didn't jive with his bohemian background story for the fans and all to go telling that tidbit everything."

"Maybe."

Stanley looks at John. "You going to bed?"

"Yeah, I'm bushed. Time change and all has gotten to me I think."

"Me too."

They reach the doors to their hotel rooms. John says, "See you in the morning." He opens his door and then turns back to Stanley. "I'm meeting a cabbie downstairs at eight. Don't be late."

"Eight A.M.?"

"Yes, A.M." John replies.

"This is looking less like a vacation to me John," Stanley complains.

"Who ever promised you a vacation?"

At exactly 8:00AM, the always punctual John Black stands in the lobby waiting on the always late Stanley Simpson. At almost 8:30, after an ignored phone call on the house phone, a tired-looking Stanley appeared in the lobby.

"It's so bloody early in this morning," Stanley complains. "Is this really necessary?"

"Sleep well did you?" John asks sarcastically.

"What little I got, yes."

"Well we're off to see Morrison's apartment." John says with marked enthusiasm.

"Swell. How do you know it still exists?" Stanley asks.

"Oh, it exists alright. There is a little map in the lobby for tourists who wish to see it."

"Wonderful," Stanley says sarcastically. "Any chance I could find a Dr. Pepper around here?"

John looks at him blankly. "What do you think?"

Stanley is disappointed but not surprised since Paris doesn't seem to have anything he likes. "Wonderful."

"Why can't you get your caffeine with coffee like the rest of the world?"

Stanley gives John a look resembling a child eating vegetables. "Because," he explains, "I don't like the taste of coffee. Isn't it enough for you that have controlled where I'm going and what I'm doing? Now you are on shaky ground going after my beverage of choice John."

Getting into a cab parked at the front of the cab stand, John gives the address to the driver. "17 Rue Beautrallis driver."

"Oui Monsieur," the cabby says as he pulls away. "Jim Morrison?" the cabby inquires.

"Oui. How did you know?" John asks.

"Oh monsieur, a very popular spot for photographers and fans. I have been there many times but you cannot go in you know."

"No?" John asks.

"No, you can only see the outside."

"Very well," John says cheerfully, "We shall have to be content with the outside then!"

Rolling his eyes, Stanley asks, "What will you gleam from that, the color of the paint?"

"Probably nothing, so we got to the gravesite earlier, that's all."

The apartment building is plain and not special in any way. The cab idles for a moment across the street from the front of the building as people speed in every direction to work and play.

"I'd take a picture, but…" John says.

"But what?" Stanley asks.

"I don't have a camera," he says sheepishly.

"You'll have to settle for a memory then won't you." Stanley says flatly. His tone turns to mocking as he says, "Some 'journalist' you are," he says making air quotes. "No camera. Sheesh!"

John looks at him and with a touch of resentment asks, "Are you always in such a bad mood early in the morning or is today something special just for me to enjoy?"

"Usually yes I am." Stanley answers rather matter-of-factly, "especially without my caffeine ritual." He looks out the window of the moving cab. "Can we get a Coke if not a Dr. Pepper? Sure they do have Coca-Cola in Paris?"

Not having listened to their entire conversation, the cab driver answers, "Oh yes, but wouldn't you prefer coffee? We have wonderful blends of coffee monsieur."

"Now this," Stanley exclaims throwing his hands in the direction of the cabbie, "this looks like a conspiracy to me John!"

"Shh, be nice." John admonishes him. "Yes driver, please take us to where there is some coffee."

"What?" Stanley loudly protests.

"They will have some sort of cola drink there too." John reassures him.

"Did I ask for some sort of cola drink? Did you really hear me say that?" Stanley asks indignantly. "No! I asked for Coca-Cola. You probably think Pepsi is the same as Coke!"

"It isn't?" John says facetiously. Off of the 'go-to-hell' look Stanley gives him, John continues, "Okay! I'll take your word for it 'oh connoisseur of the cola bean."

"No it most certainly is not! Your pissy remark not withstanding, I can tell the difference. You're just jealous because you have no taste buds apparently."

"No," John agrees, "just that useless Masters Degree in English."

"You said it. Here it is useless. You are not speaking English every time I turn around."

After traveling a block or two the cabbie pulls over at a small bistro with outside seating and a tiny window at street level where people are getting coffee and danishs to go. The cabbie turns and asks if they'd like him to get them anything while they stayed in the cab where it was warmer.

"Very nice, thank you." John says, handing a 20 Euro bill to the driver.

"We expect change!" Stanley yells as the driver exits the cab.

"Stanley, how many of these guys need to spit on you before you behave?"

"I don't know why you let him go. I'll end up with a Shasta or something. I didn't think you were that lazy."

"I'm not lazy," John says. "I wanted to talk to you about something without him hearing. He knows English you know."

"What?" Stanley asks.

"Now listen. Don't make a big deal or turn your head, but I think we have a tail."

"In the cab?"

"Yes. The same black Mercedes has been behind us since the hotel, and at the apartment it passed us and went around the corner, so I thought I was just being paranoid."

"Which you probably are," Stanley points out.

"Well it's back, and sitting three car lengths behind us down by that dress store and no one has gotten out." John moves in his seat to try to see the Mercedes. "It appears to be two men in the front. I can't tell if the back seat has anyone or not."

Stanley looks gingerly out the right back window up to the right side mirror. He can make out the fender of the car John is talking about parked behind two other cars. "You sure no one's gotten out of it?"

"No one, and when our driver gets back in and we pull away let's watch and see if that car does as well."

"Okay, no harm there I guess, but I hope you're wrong."

"Me too, but I don't think I am."

The cab driver hops back in, handing the drinks to John but interestingly enough, he hands the change to Stanley, who says, "Thank you."

Stanley grabs the bag from John to get his soda while John starts sipping his coffee.

"Wonderful blend, you were correct," John says to the cab driver. "It's very good."

Stanley pulls his bottle out of the bag to discover it is bottled water. He looks at the bottle and says, "You are the Anti-Christ, you know that."

"Why does my friend here have water monsieur?" John asks.

"Oh. They did not have any soda and he said he didn't like coffee. Did I make a mistake?"

"No, no, you were trying to help us out. Thank you."

Stanley leans over thoroughly annoyed. "You're such a pussy. Of course he made a mistake."

"Keep your voice down and pay attention to the outside." John says reminding Stanley of their unwanted tail. "Besides, water's good for you Stan so quit your bitchin' and drink some of it."

"But it doesn't wake me up and you need the water more than me anyway to wash the Xanax out of your system. It's clearly still clouding your mind."

"Whatever."

"Where to now monsieurs?" asks the cab driver.

"Pere LaChaise Cemetery please," John replies.

"Of course," he says smiling now and sending the theme in their trips.

"That's French for 'that'll be 35 more bucks suckers." Stanley says.

"Euros." John corrects him.

"Excuse me, 70 more bucks." Stanley says not taking the time to calculate the exchange rate.

"I'm paying like I told you before, and I'd like to have one cab ride in this city without being spit on. This guy clearly knows English, so shut the hell up with your attitude. Okay?"

"Okay, okay." Stanley takes a swig of water and then dozes off in the back seat while John and the cabbie chat on the half-hour ride to the cemetery.

"We're here Stanley," John says nudging him, "wake up."

"Oh goodie."

"Wait here," John tells the cabbie, "we won't be long."

"Oh monsieur, you may be there a while. There is a tour available here and…"

"Either way, wait here," John says, handing him a hundred Euro bill.

"Oui monsieur, whatever you want," he says quickly tucking it away.

"We'll never see him again John." Stanley says as they exit the cab.

"You are a negative one when it comes to human nature. He knows there's more where that came from. He'll be here when we get back." John says.

"Okay we'll see 'Mary Poppins'."

"Wrong city, that's London." John says.

"Maybe wrong city, but it's not the wrong metaphor." They approach a long line of people. "What's this line for?" Stanley asks.

"This is the line to see his grave I suppose." John answers.

"Who, Christ?" Stanley remarks. "He didn't die yesterday. Are you shitting me?"

"Shhh…" John says angrily.

The line seems to be at a virtual standstill. There are uniformed men walking up and down the side of the ropes that surround the grave.

"Is there always such a robust line?" John asks the guard on duty.

"Oh yes."

"Are you a guard or a tour guide?"

"A guard," he says looking a little deflated. "We are posted here 24 hours a day monsieur."

"Why is that?" John asks.

"All of the vandalism that has been done over the years. Relatives of people surrounding gravesites have not been happy over the years because of all the trash. Litter you know and graffiti. So we are here to keep the peace and keep it all neater I suppose."

"Posted guards and a line at a grave, now that's a hoot." Stanley says. "We are the ones alive and in a hurry. He's just lying there."

"I said shhh!" John says angrier than before. Turning back to the guard he says, "I bet you've seen some wild things here. Have you been a guard here long?"

"Yes, for 12 years now." The guard glances around and then turns back to John and says, "A few years ago when we were here, but not 24-hours a day, some vandals stole Morrison's bust from his gravestone. That's when we began the around-the-clock supervision."

"Welcome to Poet's Corner," a tour guide said as the pair make their way closer. "They named the area of the cemetery after him and other famous poets who lie in rest here," the guide continues. "He lies in an area with great literary giants like Oscar Wilde."

"Oh I see," John says, drinking it all in. "I bet you've heard all the rumors about his death?" John asks the guide.

"Oh yes, believe me, I have heard them all."

"That he is not dead for instance?" John quizzes, "or was killed?"

"Yes I've heard them all. We thought many of those rumors would end in 2001, but c'est la vie. It was not meant to be."

"What do you mean 2001?" John asks with his curiosity fully piqued.

"Well, in 2001 the lease ran out on the gravesite and he was supposed to be exhumed and sent to the U.S.A. for burial."

"What happened?" John asks.

"I don't know," the guide replies. "The French government I suppose liked that it is a tourist destination like the Eiffel Tower, so they keep him here now for all eternity I suppose."

"Hmmm, I see." John says.

The tour guide continues, "This past year, a book came out from a man who was the manager of the Rock N' Roll Circus nightclub."

"Oh yes, the underground club he supposedly frequented," John says.

"Yes. He says Morrison was overdosing in his bathroom and that some drug dealers of Morrison's took him to his apartment and put him in the tub to sober him up, and that he died there."

"But his wife, well, common-law wife Pamela Courson said that didn't happen." John interjects.

"Yes, she says they were at a movie house that night and that he overdosed that night after she fell asleep and that she found him in the bathtub." The guide shrugs their shoulders. "I guess we will never know for sure. Viva Le Mystery, eh?"

"Yeah, I guess so," John says smiling. "Does anyone come here many times over and over, or leave gifts, notes, or flowers?" John asks the guide.

"Oh, so many people leave things that the gravesite is cleared every few days."

"What happens to those items left?"

"The commissioner of the cemetery, he handles all of that. We have a work crew who takes them and bags them for the main office."

"I see." John says.

"We let flowers stay until they are dying of course, but to answer you, I don't know of any one person who comes more than another. Why do you ask?"

"Just curious."

"I have been interviewed by reporters many times, but I guess have nothing too exciting to share. Are you a reporter?" the guide asks John.

"I am writing a book about his life, yes. Have any of 'The Doors' other members come here?"

"Years ago I have heard, but not while I was ever here." The guide glances at the surroundings. "Well, we're almost next to go in," the guide says to John and about six others in line with him and Stanley. "It's behind a metal fence but you can take pictures and pay your respects," the guide says ushering them past a gate. "Enjoy."

"What an odd thing to say in a cemetery," Stanley says.

It was a simple square stone, now with flowers lining its top and around the base.

"I don't know if it is that short without a ruler," John says.

"You want to measure his grave now?" Stanley asks.

"You think they'd let me do that?"

"In a word: no. What's wrong with you?"

"I read a report from a book once that John Densmore; the drummer for 'The Doors', came here to see the grave a while after Jim was buried here, and he told the press the grave was too short to be Jim's grave."

"Too short?"

"Yeah, that's what he said."

"Well fortunately it was deep enough. Maybe he's buried on his head." Stanley muses.

"Cute. Very cute."

"That seems a little weak as far as evidence goes, don't you think? I mean, even the Roswell fans wouldn't go for that would they John?" Stanley looks at John. "Well, you know that area isn't big enough for a flying saucer to have landed in. It's just too short of a runway," Stanley jokes in a hick accent.

"If you can't contribute to the conversation and can only mock what I am saying, then just hush up because I'm trying to think."

"Of what? How many inches there are in a yard? It's 36."

"Courson once said she paid off the medical examiner to say heart attack, but only to stop the media circus that had surrounded Jimi Hendrix's and Janis Joplin's death. Does that ring true to you?"

"Don't know, don't know, could be. I guess it does make some sense."

"And her not telling the relatives until after he was buried?" John asks.

"Well you said he didn't get along with his parents. Maybe she didn't know he'd written mom again after all those years."

"Maybe, yeah."

"And that may be all if it weren't for the weirdness around those letters and us being followed and our rooms being ransacked." Stanley surmises.

"Let's go back to the hotel," John says. "I need to call some more of our leads."

"Oh goodie, the circus continues."

"The guy last night was quite normal Stanley."

"Yeah, I guess so."

"You, on the other hand 'Mr. Dion'…"

"Just trying to stay interested and alert that's all." They start walking away from the gravesite. As they get to the front of the cemetery Stanley suddenly says, "Well I'll be damned!"

"What Stanley? Did you notice something significant?"

"Yes I did," Stanley answers. "The cabbie did stay where you told him to wait for us."

John rolls his eyes as they get into their waiting taxi. "Do you see, you know who anywhere Stan?" John asks.

"No, you John?" Stanley answers, knowing he was referring to the car following earlier.

"No, but keep your eyes peeled," John says.

John instructs the cabbie to take them back to the Ritz. Two streets away from arriving at the hotel, John spots the Mercedes again in traffic behind them. "Stanley," he says nudging him and pointing at the side mirror.

"Crap! You think that's our buddies?"

"Yes I do," he answers.

The car continues to follow them all the way back to the hotel, where it speeds around a corner and out of sight past their cab. As they get out of the taxi, John tells the cabbie to keep the change but to give him a card in case they want to call on him again, which the driver gladly does, considering John's generosity.

As John bends inside the cab to talk, he notices the Mercedes coming back up the street and pulls to the curb down the block and parks.

The pair goes into the hotel and straight to John's room to look over phone messages. "Stanley," John says, "the Mercedes slowed past the hotel then went a block away down another street, then came back and sat at the curb down the street from here."

"Did you ever think that maybe it's just a rival reporter or news organization?"

"Actually yes, I have thought that's possible. But in the U.S. it couldn't be that now, could it?"

"Well I agree someone was following us there, but is it possible this tail is about your news conference and not about the letters?" Stanley asks.

"Yes, I suppose, and until we find out something conclusive, we can only speculate. " John notices a large piece of paper on the floor near the room's front door along with more messages. "The hotel is charging me because I'm getting so many calls."

"How very French of them," Stanley comments. "Still probably need the dough after World War II and all. Lots to repair I heard."

John looks at the smirk on Stanley's face. "You don't care about karma at all do you?"

"My karma ran over my dogma a long time ago John."

"Well, this one is either nuts or promising," John says waving one of the memo sheets in the air. "It's a guy named Phoenix who says he'd like to 'compare notes' with us and that he knows the truth, whatever that means. Obviously he wants to pique my curiosity."

"Which I'm sure he did."

"Yes he did. Doesn't it pique yours?"

"No. He is probably just another book writer or some such like last night." Stanley says.

"Probably, but you never know unless you meet them!"

"You're gonna call. I know you are, so go ahead."

John was, in fact, already dialing the phone by the bed. "Hello. Yes, Mr. Phoenix? Yes, Mr. Jonathan Black here. Fine, thank you. Listen, we have been meeting people that have leads for us at this little bar near here… What? Seriously Mr. Phoenix, I don't see how we need that sort of… Yes? Yes?"

"What?" Stanley asks, leaning in to try and hear the phone conversation.

"Shh," John hisses at him. "Well okay, if you insist. 11AM it is." John says, hanging up the phone.

"You're a pushover you know that. Insist on what?" Stanley asks.

"How many times have I got to tell you how hard it is to hear someone on the phone while you are squawking in the background?"

"So where are we going now? At 11AM I hear."

"Tomorrow at 11AM we're going on some boat tour on the River Seine. He seemed a bit paranoid that's for sure, and he asked me did I think we have ever been followed in our investigation."

"What did you say to that?"

"I said yes."

"Why?"

"Well, if he's working for the bad guys, why lie? If he's not, why not make him feel at home? He sounded like being followed was what worried him most and I wanted him to feel comfortable."

"I know it's a long shot, but what if he really knows something?"

"I'm going to call some more of these leads back and make some more appointments."

"Can't wait," Stanley says sarcastically. "I'm going next door to order a pizza or something that is even remotely American."

"Stanley, honey…"

"Yes baby doll?" Stanley asks as he starts walking to the door.

"Pizza is not American. It's…never mind."

"When I want to learn something I will pick up a book."

"Until then, bon appetit!"

"You do that just to piss me off. I know you do."

"Okay, but get back here soon. We have an early morning of it."

"11AM is not early, thank you for that. At least it's better than today."

"Well yeah, about that… I agree 11AM is not too early, but I want to go to the Paris library first at 8AM."

"I hate you. Why do you insist on doing things so early in the damn morning?" Stanley asks agitated. "Never mind, whatever your reason it's not going to be good enough for me anyway. Goodnight!" Stanley slams the door as he leaves John to return phone calls and set up more appointments.

CHAPTER ELEVEN

Morning breaks amidst foggy weather and a light drizzle of rain. John wonders if the boat tour will still go on as planned. It looks like the rain is only going to get heavier but the front desk bell captain said the boat has lower decks and inside compartments and goes on tour – rain or shine.

"Stanley! You slept well I trust?" John asks as he appears in the dining room the next morning.

"Well actually no. I tossed and turned a lot. I think it was the pizza I had last night, and wipe that smirk off your face. It isn't funny. I was on the toilet from 2AM to…"

"Okay, okay, I'm not your doctor. I get the picture," John says interrupting him. "I called two other leads back last night by the way but they sounded like crack pots."

"Oh, and the boat guy didn't?" Stanley asks with pointed sarcasm.

"Well, he sounded paranoid but then sometimes paranoid is really just a well informed instinct. Someone was following us a couple of times you know, and if this guy knows something…anything…maybe someone has followed him too, so it couldn't hurt to hear him out."

"Why? Do you think he plays bridge with Mrs. Birch on Sundays, or maybe he buys stray Jim Morrison letters on the black market? Or even better, maybe he holds irresponsible press conferences about shit he knows nothing about."

"Oh I get it," John says, "it's me you're referring to."

"Is this the last lead?" Stanley impatiently asks.

"Yes. Unless someone else calls that sounds plausible." John replies.

The pair leaves their breakfast barely touched and walks out to the street level cab stand again. John waves to the bellman and tips him a few Euros.

"Why must you always throw money away on stupid things like that?"

"The man hailed our cab and stands all day in the rain. He deserves a tip." John explains.

"The Euro is twice the dollar you know. You gave the man too much."

"You can be so cheap sometimes, channeling that inner banker of yours. It was my money so drop it."

The taxi takes them first to the Paris library, which is housed in a beautiful centuries-old building in the heart of the city, its architecture full of marble and columns with large griffins adorning the buildings outside.

"What a beautiful library," Stanley says. "You know John; the one near my house is in a converted trailer. Truly," Stanley says while John stares at him.

"No one cherishes older architecture anymore Stanley," John tells him. "In Europe, something two-hundred-years-old isn't even considered that old. Their history is centuries older than our little country, no matter how influential we may have become."

The pair ascends the stairs and walks into the library's main hall where John asks an older woman behind the periodical counter where their microfiche is kept. She points them to a back section where rows of tiny microfiche viewers run down one wall, each with their own little cubby. It was a system where you look up the subject in a card file and then write your selection down on a small memo pad. You then give it to a library helper, who gets the reel for you and places it into the machine. If you need to print anything you see, you place 50 cents in Euros into the machine's front and out it would come, as simple as that.

The first few mentions of Morrison's death, etc, for nearly thirty minutes yielded nothing new to John's eyes until: "Look here on this microfiche of a newspaper," he said drawing Stanley's attention to it. "July 3, 1971, Jim Morrison was found dead in a bathtub. July 3rd, one day before Independence Day."

"Yes, that's true, hmm, so?"

"Buried at Pere LaChaise in Paris." John continues. "Another article here says in 1990 someone stole his headstone."

Stanley perks up. "Now that's some memorabilia we could've sold for some money John!"

"Could you try and stay focused?"

"You stay focused. This is all stuff we already know, so why did you call me over here?"

"On April 25, 1974, Pamela Courson died of an overdose. A famous interviewer at the time, who says he also got letters from Paris, wrote about her death, how she was Jim's common law wife."

"Yada, yada, yada. Again I say, so what?"

"The writer has a byline and address here in Paris, and 1990 wasn't so long ago. Maybe he's still at this address. Let's go try and see this guy. We have no other leads except our 11AM guy on the boat, or if whoever followed us and ransacked our rooms pops up again right?"

"Well that goes without saying if you call someone following up a lead."

"Yes I do."

Stanley waves his arm in a sweeping motion. "Okay, like I keep telling you, it's your circus, and you're the head clown so whatever. Lead on…"

"Thanks for the charming metaphor Stanley," John says as they leave the building and hail another cab.

John hands the cab driver a slip of paper he copied in the library and says, "Driver, this address please."

"Oui," the cabbie replies.

It's not long before they arrive at a row of lovely brownstone buildings with small gardens between them in a nice part of town.

"Well," John says, "he appears to make a living as a writer." He looks up at the buildings. "These don't look too shabby."

As with the others, they leave the cab driver with a 100 Euro bill to wait on them and climb the steps of one of the buildings. Searching for the writer's name, John finds it on a box to the left of the front door. Ringing the buzzer at the brownstone, John is excited that the man still lives there and hopes he's home.

"Mr. Flannigan?" John speaks into the intercom.

"Yes?" The voice responds.

"I'm Mr. Black, Jonathan Black, and I'm with my associate Mr. Stanley Simpson. We are writers for a book concerning the death of rock star Jim Morrison."

"So? What has this to do with me?" he asks, sounding irritated.

"I have a different view of events of his last days here in Paris and I read in an old newspaper article that you may agree with me. Can we speak to you? I promise to be brief."

No answer comes from the intercom. Just as John looks at Stanley in a defeated way, the door buzzes. John and Stanley enter the building and walk to Flannigan's apartment. In the hallway at Flannigan's door, John is about to tell Stanley to behave when the door swings open widely and Flannigan is already talking to them.

"Jim wasn't into destroying himself, although he was an alcoholic." Flannigan says immediately after ushering John and Stanley into his apartment. He holds out his hand and says, "I'm Jack Flannigan, but you already know that don't you?" John and Stanley both shake his hand and take a seat in chairs across from his sofa.

"I got eight to ten letters from him while he was in Paris. They were somber and laced with despair. I was on assignment in Chicago and later Washington covering the Vietnam unrest. The last letter he mailed to me was only a few days before his overdose. He said in it that he was tired and misunderstood. I personally believe Pam, in an effort to hook him on heroin and harder stuff like she was into, killed him. Perhaps accidentally like John Belushi's girlfriend did years later with him, and the grief and knowledge of that drove her to kill herself later."

"The official report on his death though was heart attack at age 27, not typical for alcoholism," John says to Jack.

"No but typical for a drug overdose like heroin."

"Without an autopsy we may never know," John says.

"True, true. I still have a file on him. If it helps your investigation at all, you are welcome to it, but I think it's nothing groundbreaking. Just routine information," he says, opening a filing cabinet and handing over a thick manila file to John.

John opens the file to the front page and begins reading. "Born in Florida on December 8, 1943, father was Steve Morrison; a U.S. Admiral in the Navy. Damn that's impressive. Did most people know that?" John asks.

"No, he didn't along with his straight-laced parents and rarely spoke of them in interviews."

"Did you know that Stanley?" John asks.

"Are you speaking to me?" Stanley says, looking back from the window he was staring out of.

"Sorry, what was I thinking...?" John says, going back to the notes. "High IQ, said to be 149. His alter ego he named 'The Lizard King'.

"Fun facts John, are we done here?" Stanley asks impatiently.

"Don't be rude Stanley." John says disapprovingly. Looking back to the file John continues, "Pamela Courson was considered his common law wife. He called her his 'cosmic mate' in a letter once to a friend. Although he was said to have an affair with Linda Ashcroft from 1967 to 1971."

"And don't forget Patricia Kennealy in 1969, whom he married in 1970." Jack adds.

"He had a way with the ladies huh?" Stanley says, sounding more interested. "Cosmic mates do that sort of thing you know," he says mockingly.

"Oh, now you respect him?" John asks. "All rock stars seem to fall into that trap. The mass adoration and easy beautiful women must be hard to resist," John says thinking aloud.

"Why resist?" Stanley asks.

"What's all this abut some low budget film in the file here?" John asks Jack.

"Yes," Jack replies, "it was called 'Beyond the Doors' and advanced the theory that he and Hendrix and Joplin were killed by a government set out to stamp out radicals."

"Really?" John asks, his interest piqued.

"Yes, but they had no connections, no proof, it was pure crap."

"When did Janis die?" John asks.

"Joplin died October 4, 1970."

"And Hendrix?"

"Hendrix died September 18, 1970. Did you know Hendrix was an Army paratrooper?"

"Really?"

"101st Airborne, but was discharged two years before Vietnam broke out."

"How convenient," Stanley snorts.

"Monika Danneman, Jimi Hendrix's girlfriend was with him the last night he was alive. She said he was alive and in an ambulance on the way to the hospital when he died of a drug overdose. This was the 60s remember; free love and cheap drugs with lots of experimenting. Published reports were different though. They say he was dead and the apartment was empty when the ambulance arrived, but if that was the case, who called the ambulance? Certainly not a dead man." Jack notes and then adds, "By the way, in 1996, Danneman took her own life as well, an apparent suicide."

"Really..." John says.

"Are you going to keep saying that?" Stanley asks. "Look, Jim was a cursed soul huh? That much I believe some people are." Stanley interjects.

"You believe in curses?" Jack asks.

Stanley answers, "Look, I know chicks can get wrapped up in a boy, but two of them off themselves that had a relationship with him?"

"No Stanley," John says, "the other one had a relationship with Hendrix."

"Maybe he was just a great guy," Stanley says ignoring John. "I'd love to think a woman would kill herself over me." Stanley muses.

"That's a goal for you?" John asks.

"Not a goal really, just very romantic. Very 'Romeo and Juliet' you know."

John looks at Stanley. "They killed themselves because they couldn't be together, not because one couldn't commit to a monogamous relationship."

"Couldn't commit. Oh, that's supposed to be me is it? Oh, I get it, funny John funny." Stanley looks to Jack. "Do they have an open mike night at a comedy club near here Mr. Flannigan?"

"Excuse us a moment Mr. Flannigan," John says as he pulls Stanley out of his chair. Taking him to another part of the office, John lowers his voice. "We are supposed to be a team and you are being an asshole and obnoxious. Unprofessional for a pair of journalists."

"We are not journalists, remember?"

"But he doesn't know that and we need to appear to be legit. Okay?"

"Alright, alright, calm down," Stanley says.

Walking back into the room with Mr. Flannigan, John says, "Mr. Flannigan, thank you so much for your notes. We will of course credit you in our book for anything we use from your research. If you think of anything else, here's my number," John says, handing him a business card. "Please don't hesitate to call me. While we are in Paris, we're staying at the Ritz on the Champs-Élysées."

"Of course Mr. Black, of course." Jack says as he closes his apartment door.

Once outside and climbing back into the cab, Stanley says, "Did that glean you anything new?"

"No, not really, but some of the background information is interesting. I doubt it has very much bearing on everything that's going on." John replies.

"Ah! A crack of sanity starting to peek in," Stanley teases. "And what if the guy we're meeting next is a bust, then what?"

"Okay, I'll tell you what. If the next guy doesn't give us any new leads, I'll pack it in."

"Promise?" Stanley asks.

"Yes I promise."

CHAPTER TWELVE

About 20 minutes later, the taxi pulls up to a boat landing where tourists in line are starting to board the boat. "Thank goodness I called up the cab again, that I tipped with that 100 spot," John says. "I don't know how to reach this guy and we almost missed the boat."

"200 spot," Stanley corrects. "You keep forgetting the conversion rate. How the hell are we supposed to know when we meet this guy? I mean, what does he look like?"

"Interesting part about that. He said he would recognize us from our little impromptu press conference."

"Swell. If the weather were better with some visibility I could at least enjoy the tour, but if this guy is a no-show, this could be a total mess." Stanley says as they hand their tickets over to a man and step onto the boat's deck.

"Well it's not raining for the moment, so let's stay up on the top deck and make it easier for him to find us."

As John and Stanley stand on the deck, someone walks up behind them and stands next to them at the railing. "Thank you for coming Mr. Black. I wasn't sure you would."

John turns and sees a man that appears to be in his sixties standing there. He's tanned and in good shape, handsome, but looking very worried or tired. "Yeah, well, your little chat with me intrigued me to say the least." John says while shaking his hand. Turning to Stanley he says, "This is my associate, Mr. Stanley Simpson."

"Yes, your investigations intrigued me as well. I read about them in the papers here," he says while absentmindedly shaking Stanley's hand. "Tell me something Mr. Black. Do you really believe those old rock stars were snuffed out like you told one of the reporters at the conference?"

"Forgive me Mr. Phoenix was it?" John says, "Like the city in Arizona?"

"Something like that, yes," the man replies.

"Okay Mr. Phoenix, you told me you had something of interest to tell me. I didn't come here to be interviewed by you or anyone else. Besides, I told the press no such thing. It was only one of the many theories we discussed."

Sensing John was annoyed, the man tried smoothing things over. "Stay cool man, stay cool. I am on your side, okay?"

"What is your interest in my 'investigations' as you called them?"

"I may be able to help you with a critical piece of the puzzle involving one of the cats in your investigation."

"Which one?"

"Which one what?" Stanley interrupts, "And why are we talking about cats now?"

"He means people. It's slang Stanley. If you can't keep up at least keep quiet." John says.

"Who is he again?" Mr. Phoenix asks, pointing at Stanley.

"He's a partner in my investigations," John replies.

"A reluctant partner," Stanley interjects.

"Reluctant meaning you're scared, or you don't believe in Mr. Black's theory?"

"Nothing to be scared about, just not a believer in all of this nonsense." Stanley responds.

"I see. Well, Mr. Simpson I can assure you there is something to be scared of. Or at least there used to be," he says more hesitantly as he looks down.

"Used to be?" John asks.

"Years ago, a government operative or hell, maybe a whole handful of them caused the death of a famous rock star, maybe even more than one."

"Can you prove what you are saying?" John asks.

"I know about the night one of them died. Wouldn't that be of help?" Mr. Phoenix answers.

"Yes of course it would," John says anxiously. "Which one?"

"Jim Morrison."

"Well what do you know that could help us?"

"You probably know that the press said Pamela Courson found him dead and then got a local doctor to come over to his Paris flat and pronounce him dead, then off to a quickie cremation and voila, end of Jim."

"Yes, that's the accepted truth." John says.

"Well truth, like art, is in the eye of the beholder isn't it Mr. Black?"

"Perhaps... I asked you what you knew but so far we've only reviewed known facts. Mr. Phoenix, were you involved somehow?"

"Somehow..." he says cryptically. "Here's what you need to know. Have you tried to look up the doctor who signed the death certificate?"

"Yes," John replies. "No one knows what happened to him actually. If he was over 40 at the time then he'd be 80 now and may possibly even be dead by now."

"Yeah maybe, or did it occur to you that maybe he never really existed in the first place?" Mr. Phoenix asks, raising one eyebrow.

John shakes his head. "That doesn't seem conceivable. I mean, who would have helped Pamela, dispose of the body? Not just anyone can cremate a body you know."

Mr. Phoenix nods in agreement. "True, but what if, and I know this sounds far-fetched, but try and follow me on this, okay?"

"Okay, but if this is just a theory we are discussing, that you have no proof on, I have a bag full of theories and more important things to do right now than discuss them with a man who I don't even know and claims to be 'Mr. Phoenix' from Phoenix."

"I never said I was from Phoenix. I said the name was like the city," he says correcting John.

I don't know if you're here to try and pick my brain on my progress, or to really be helpful and if helpful, why? It's all those pesky journalistic questions you know, who, what, when, where, and why Mr. Phoenix."

John starts walking away from the railing. "I'm sorry, but I think I need to go. I appreciate your interest in all of this."

"Wait Mr. Black," Phoenix says, "and in ten minutes time I promise you one thing; you will be awfully glad you waited. Besides, this boat won't dock for another 45 minutes."

John turns back to the railing and says, "Five minutes, not ten Mr. Phoenix, to gain my interest."

"Mr. Black, what if I told you Jim Morrison felt like his life was in danger?"

"How did you come up with that little line of thinking Mr. Phoenix? I gathered as much from information I have uncovered on my own, but I want to know how you came to that conclusion."

"Oh, you mean the letters that sold at C&R's auction house last week?"

"Yes, then you know about them?" John asks.

"Yes, and you were a bidder?" Phoenix asks.

"Yes," John answers.

"Did you secure them?"

"No."

"Did you read them?"

"No," John says, glaring at Stanley to shut up and not betray anything. "I'm only aware that Morrison may have been frightened for his safety. And so?"

"And so, he was frightened and the night in question…"

"The night he died?" John asks.

"Yes, let's say for the sake of a good storyline he was kicked back in his apartment with his girlfriend."

"Pamela?"

"Yes, Pamela, and a new male friend he had met earlier as well."

"A threesome?"

"Yes."

Not believing what he's hearing, John holds up a hand. "Stop right there."

"Why?" Phoenix asks.

"There is no mention of anyone else being with Morrison that night. Published reports have suggested that he went to a movie alone and a club where some believe he really overdosed."

"Oh yes," he says with recognition. "The theory is that Pamela got his body back to the apartment, into the tub, and then called the ambulance."

"Yes."

"And you believe that was possible without anyone else to help her?"

John throws caution to the wind. "Okay, so let's say as you did, that for the sake of this conversation, another male was present the night he died. You think this unidentified and unknown to history man killed him?"

"Nope," Mr. Phoenix replies.

"Okay, go on then." John says.

"They are just drinking. Chillin', nothing harder than booze and some weed, and late, late in the night, someone else shows up."

"A fourth person?" John asks.

"Yes."

"Male or female?"

"Male."

"Who?"

"Don't know," Mr. Phoenix says with a shrug, "because the occupants of the apartment are all asleep."

"You mean someone breaks in?" John asks.

"Yes," Mr. Phoenix answers.

Trying to make sense out of what he's being told, John recaps, "Someone with a syringe of a lethal substance sticks Jim. He dies quietly in his sleep, all while the others remain passed out?"

"Yes."

"Hard sell I think."

"And the killer leaves the scene."

Not able to come to terms with it, John shakes his head and says, "Okay Mr. Phoenix. I'm not saying something like this isn't possible but forgive me, there are too many loose ends. Like why not kill Pamela for one?"

"She was asleep, and two overdoses in one night would've been harder to believe and brought more attention. Police even in France can't ignore a double death. Besides, that would look too romantic, like a suicide pact when the intention was to discredit and not martyr."

"Okay, wild theory. And the other guy that was there was in on it?"

"No, also passed out."

"And you found this out from the unidentified guy?"

"In a way yes. Let me finish." Phoenix says. "The girlfriend, Pamela, wakes up and calls the doctor because the guy is lying there looking very dead."

"And the third male, he would be coming to by now, yes?"

"Well…"

"See, this is where it comes off the tracks Mr. Phoenix," John says. "Pamela naturally would've awakened him. He would've also come forward by now, and we know that Pamela never dated anyone seriously after Jim's death, and before her own."

"Yes, she also overdosed years later. I know. But, maybe she didn't overdose any more than Morrison did."

"So you think someone killed her because she might have known something?" John asks.

"No. They killed her because they knew she knew something." Phoenix insists.

"But if the killer knew he had gotten away clean without waking the other two, why risk killing her and so many years later at that? Especially since the motive was to kill Morrison only you said, and the person had ample opportunity to kill her that same night."

"Yes, I agree, the killer did originally think he had done is deed unseen."

"You mean someone did see him?" John asks.

"Yes."

"The third guy?"

"Sort of."

John is becoming frustrated listening to Mr. Phoenix's version of events. "Now that can't be right. You don't watch someone get murdered and lay quiet enough to fool the trained killer with the syringe. No, still doesn't have a ring of truth to it. I'm sorry Mr. Phoenix. I mean you do tell your story with a sense of authority, I give you that much, but unless the punch line is that you are the third man in the apartment that night, I think I will still need to be going."

"No, I am not the third guy."

"Of course not," Stanley says. "This guy may be just trying to throw us off the track you know John."

"True Stanley, true." John turns to Mr. Phoenix. "I don't suppose you'd like to show me identification that says you are in fact someone named Phoenix?"

"No, I wouldn't…couldn't actually, even if I wanted to."

"Exactly," John says starting to walk away from the conversation for the second time.

"Did you at least meet or know the third guy? Is that where your information comes from?" Stanley asks impatiently.

"Yes I knew him."

"Is he alive today?" John asks.

"No."

"Before he died, he gave you this information then?" John surmises.

"Something like that," Mr. Phoenix replies.

"Well 'something like that' just doesn't get it for me Mr. Phoenix. I'm afraid I'm in search of facts, not some second party deathbed confession no offense to your friend. I'm sure you were very close."

"Not really." Taking one last stab at it, Mr. Phoenix says, "Let me put a finer point on it for you Mr. Black."

"Please do," John says, now with a bit of sarcasm.

"The killer is in a darkened apartment where he is expecting to find, according to his information, two people: one woman and one man."

"But he finds three, so you say," John says.

"No, Mr. Black, he finds two, just as he expected he would."

"What? Now you lost me again."

"He finds two because unexpectedly, one had awakened just before the killer arrived and was in another room. When he hears the killer enter, he hides and watches the whole thing in horror."

"Okay, so we are back to your friend again, the third guy."

"No, you really just aren't following me Mr. Black."

"I'm also done playing games with you Mr. Phoenix. You're talking in riddles and circles, and since you cannot or will not tell me your involvement in all of this, or give me information I can use, I really must say goodbye this time."

"You need to trust me Mr. Black and stop and think this through," Mr. Phoenix says, now visibly agitated and trying to keep his voice down while looking furtively about the deck. I know what happened that night Mr. Black, to some extent anyway."

"Then Mr. Phoenix, either you are the third guy or you knew the third guy, or you are the killer. Which is it?"

"No, no, and no."

"No what?" John asks, now angrier than before.

"No to all three."

"Then you are guessing or dealing in even more far removed hearsay and while I appreciate your enthusiasm, I really must…"

"Mr. Black," Phoenix interrupts.

"I really must be going Mr. Phoenix." John rises from his chair.

"Mr. Black," he says again more insistently this time.

"I'm sorry Mr. Phoenix." John looks to Stanley. "Stanley, let's go."

"Mr. Black!" he says a third time, firmer and louder in tone. "I never said I wasn't there that night. I said I wasn't the third guy."

John suddenly fell back into his seat as if he himself was shot with a syringe. Leaning forward, he looks at Mr. Phoenix and in a stifled whisper asks, "Are you telling me that you did in fact kill Jim Morrison Mr. Phoenix?"

John's mind reels at the prospect that he is face-to-face with the killer of one of the most influential rock singers of all time when he can't even prove to the world a murder existed. He feels frightened for the first time, really frightened, and wonders if he should flee the boat. But how could he? He looks at Stanley, whose face is white as a ghost.

Time seems to stand still for a moment while a sly smile begins to spread across Mr. Phoenix's face. It is a disturbing expression. John starts thinking that perhaps they'll be killed next for snooping. *Yes, that has to be it. This must be the letter buyer, the guy who has been following us in the cars.*

Phoenix breaks the awkward silence and says, "I'm so glad after all these years, someone finally began to suspect foul play and put this together instead of thinking Morrison was alive and had faked his death or was a simple overdose case."

John can hardly believe he's hearing what Phoenix is saying. "Well, I never really believed those theories either."

"But you do believe he was killed?" Phoenix asks.

"Well, yes, especially since you just admitted to it."

"To being the killer?" Phoenix asks matter of factly.

"Well yes."

Phoenix shakes his head. "I did nothing of the kind. I am not the killer, and truthfully, I am not sure who was, but I do believe he was government placed."

"What?" John asks, thoroughly surprised.

"Mr. Black, you look surprised at the thought that our government could do such a thing."

"Not really. I'm just terribly confused, or lost again, in your story."

"I see that," Phoenix says chuckling for a moment. "No Mr. Black, I don't mean to make light of your research. I contacted you because of your research, and because maybe you can solve this crime that has been unsolved for so long."

"Then why were you laughing, if not at me?" John demands.

"I was laughing because it never occurred to me that you would misunderstand me as badly as you have."

"Misunderstood you? How?"

"Yes Mr. Black. I thought you understood me earlier when I said that I was not the killer or the third man in the apartment that night."

"Understand what? What's to understand?"

Mr. Phoenix sits up in his chair and with a seriously sobering expression says, "That I am, in fact, Jim Morrison."

CHAPTER THIRTEEN

"THE Jim Morrison?" John finally stutters after what seems like an eternity.

"Well I'm not Jim, Jr.; although I'm fairly sure there may be a few of them floating around out there. I kinda had the hopes that that 'Creed' singer was my son. What's his name again?"

"Scott Stapp," John says almost absentmindedly.

"Yeah, him." Morrison says.

"You like him Mr. Phoenix?" John asks.

"Not necessarily. I just think he copied a lot of my style and I hoped he came by it honestly. But seriously, I think he's too young to be mine."

"I'm sure it's more the case of stealing your moves, or imitating, I mean," Stanley says.

"Influenced by," John interrupts, "is more polite."

"Yes, you don't say stealing," Jim says. "The Music Industry is even tougher today than when I came up in it. On that subject, it used to be the only ones stealing music were the record labels."

"Countless artists must..." John says.

"Must what? Steal?" Jim asks.

"No, be influenced by your work." John replies.

"Okay, so you just believe he's who he says he is?" Stanley looks at John in shock and back to Jim in disbelief. "How about an ID fella. John, even I know he's not going to be packing a driver's license with Jim Morrison on it if he is who he says he is."

"Thank you Mr. Black, for the comment about my work influencing others." Jim says, ignoring Stanley.

"Christ, you're talking to him like he's…"

"Jim Morrison?" John asks.

"Yes!" Stanley shouts back.

"Hold your voice down Stanley," John says looking around the deck area.

"I'm sure this is all very unsettling for you both, odd in fact." Jim says.

"No," Stanley answers, "Anna Nicole was odd. This is creepy."

"I'm creepy to you?" Jim asks, sounding a bit offended.

"No, I meant…" Stanley says flustered.

"I think I understand," John says looking back and forth between Jim and Stanley. "Can we go on wit this talk though more to the subject anyway? I have so many questions."

"I'm sure you do," Jim starts, "as I do actually, so let's say we trade information, and let's stop talking out here." He looks around suspiciously. "If someone is following you like you alluded to on the phone with me, and I believe you, then it's risky for us to stay out here any longer, even more so for me."

"Yes of course, I understand," John says.

The trio goes downstairs to the bar/restaurant area and finds a booth in the back to sit in. As soon as they sit, John continues the conversation. "Jim," John says, hesitating for a beat in the newness of it all, "I'm a bit of a handwriting expert. Could you sign your name on this napkin for me?"

"Like I did all those years ago or like I do now?" Jim asks.

"Good point. Handwriting changes slightly every six months or so for everyone, but there would be some points still the same."

"Well my friend, we have had a lot of six months go by."

"Can you sign like you did, you know, back then?"

"Sure." Jim scribbles on the napkin.

John observes him signing the paper and then takes a closer look at the signature. "Here's something you can appreciate Stanley," he says while handing Stanley the napkin. "That's worth a couple of thousand bucks."

"Really? Cause we're in the hole on this trip," Stanley says while getting up.

"Stanley, where are you going?" John asks.

"To the bar for a pile of napkins."

"Sit down. I was merely making a point," John says, taking the napkin back.

"But he and you said," Stanley says looking more confused than ever.

"Shut up," John says. He turns his attention back to Jim. "Jim, where have you been for all this time?"

"Brazil," he answers, "for quite a long time. It's a regular odditorium down there. Nazi war criminals, convicts, embezzlers, porn kingpins, drug dealers, deposed royalty, and me," he says smiling. "I think even the Loch Ness monster beat fins down there until the heat died down on him, or her."

"I always thought it was a her, 'Nessie' you know." Stanley says smiling.

"Could be," Jim says while returning the smile.

"Do you believe everything you read in print Stanley?" John asks.

"No, not everything."

"Once when were in high school, do you remember the time we found out someone had written your name on the bathroom wall with the phrase 'for a good time call'?"

"Yes I do. Good times, good times." Stanley recalls.

"Well I didn't believe that and it was in print."

"Hate the game, not the player John, and you don't have to be an asshole to make a point." Stanley says annoyed.

"No, but I find that it's remembered better when I am."   Returning to his conversation, "Jim, what happened? Who killed you, or thought they did anyway?"

"It was like I told you only I got up to take a piss and watched from a back room while this guy, I never saw his face, came into the apartment. I thought at first that he was partier, maybe even a fan, but then when I caught glimpses of him, he looked like a doctor with a bag and all. He pulled out a syringe and injected this cat we had come home with that we met partying at a club called the Rock N' Roll Circus."

"So you were there? People are now saying they saw you there on drugs." John says.

"Yes, people paid to say things or with faulty memories or that like the limelight. Who knows at this point what their motivations were. We were all so naïve back then, I mean we represented a mistrustful nation of youth who collectively knew not the trust 'the man'." Jim says doing air quotations with his fingers. "But in truth, we had no idea what 'the man' was truly capable of."

"The man," Stanley mouthed to John with a look of confusion.

"Establishment, the government, really Stanley, how old are you?"

Jim continues, "I mean the government – or someone – wanted to make examples out of all of us who had a higher profile. Any of us with any kind of influence over the youth to some degree, I guess. We'd all been warned J. Edgar Hoover had files on us as subversives! Even Paul McCartney was deported for marijuana use briefly in those days, but today? Hell, he's been knighted by the Queen for crying out loud. My point is…"

"I get your point," John says. "They were turbulent times; times of war, most of the nation didn't understand why kids were dying in Vietnam. Today, sadder still, most people still don't." John adds ruefully.

"The rich, younger singers were protesting a war they never had to fight in," Jim says in agreement. "I would've fought if I thought we were fighting for any of the right reasons, and I only made my record company rich by the way.

"Not me, but our country was founded on civil liberties – freedom of speech. Maybe that holds for you, but when someone has a mass following of young impressionable people like we did, a generation really, they need to show a sense of responsibility in this message."

"How long were you in Brazil?" John asks.

"I hid down there about five years, three of them drunk off my ass."

"How did you survive?"

"First Pam wired me money. She got some from my parents at first."

"They knew you were alive?"

"Hell no, they just felt sorry for her, thought the dough was for funeral stuff I guess, but they got ugly quick with each other and started fighting over control of my music with the other guys in 'The Doors'. I had insurance money too, and thank God I made her beneficiary! So she cremated Michael; that was the cat's name that was killed that night. No one ever looked for him. It was the sixties remember, and he had already spent years in some commune. His parents had lost track of him long before. Thank God he wasn't married or had any kids."

"Did you continue to write music?"

"No. Poetry some, but not even that for years. I taught English in Brazil, if you can imagine that. They didn't need any degree, just someone who knew English. I picked up Spanish pretty quickly. For money, I hooked up with some rich broads who idolized Morrison and thought I looked like him."

"Now we're talking!" Stanley says as he perks up to listen to more.

"Really Stanley, calm down. It's his story not yours."

"I wasn't proud of that," Jim continues, "but I had no choice, you know. It took years for me to get some good looking, passable credentials together, which was easier then than now from what I understand, and then I re-entered the U.S. with the name Richard Phoenix."

"Rising from the ashes," John says, the story of the mythical bird not escaping his notice.

"Yeah, pretty cute huh? I almost made a name out of my name's letters."

"Like Mo Jo Risin; another anagram you once used?"

"Yes, but I thought that could be found out too easily. What a reality check it all was for me. I would never say I was naïve, but this was a whole 'nother ballgame, you know?"

"No, I can't even imagine," John says.

"Well you better start imagining it because whoever's been following you may be my guy."

"We don't know who is following us or why."

Stanley shifts in his chair and leans in to nudge John's arm. "Government plates, remember?"

"Christ! It's government following you two?" Jim exclaims.

"In the states, in Los Angeles, we saw government plates on a car that was following us, but that doesn't prove anything." John says glaring at Stanley.

"I always felt like it was government," Jim says.

"Did you ever see Pam again?" John asks, trying to change the subject.

"She started rumors after a while that I had faked my death and was alive. It helped I guess that I mentioned in an article once that I might do that to escape fame. She had an ulterior motive though. She thought she would be able to come to be with me, but I didn't want to risk her life, and running her mouth might have done that. So I got a friend in Brazil to call her and say I had died in a car crash and that they only found her name and number on me. She said she didn't know who I was, but he told me she broke down and cried on the phone." Jim looks down at the table. "I did it to protect her."

"She bought it?" John asks.

"Sometimes I thought so, other times no. Under the circumstances I could see how she may not have bought it, you know?" He tilts his head and continues talking. "She had trouble, heroin addictions you know, and with me 'dead', I thought she overdosed. It might have been legitimate but now I'm not so sure."

He takes a deep breath, as if trying to reconcile the past or even justify it to himself. "So anyway, like I was saying, I didn't feel it was safe to go back to Paris and I didn't want to look up my folks. My dad was in the military and I thought the government was in on this, so I went as far as I could in the U.S. – Florida. It was the late 70s."

"You had lived there growing up, hadn't you?"

"Yes I had. I started over best I could can you believe as a printer?"

"Sure, why not?"

"Actually, over the years I got pretty good at it and built a few locations. My own little chain..." Jim smiles at his accomplishment. "I sold the stores years later and thought that, as they say, was that."

"But?" John asks.

"Yes but... Out of the blue, I got an IRS audit this past year stating something wasn't quite right with my social security number, etc. I thought my long ago identity may have been compromised. Maybe paranoid perhaps, but under my circumstances..."

"I understand completely."

"I'd always done my own accounting all those years, and I was trying to decide if I should calm down and show up, or split again when I read in the paper about my letters coming up at auction. I tried to remember what all I had written to my mother all those years ago but couldn't. I called and found out that they had sold for so much, but to an anonymous buyer. That kind of freaked me out some more.
I called back a few times but they wouldn't ever tell me anything, but they did tell me you two guys were writing a book about me."

Stanley and John look at each other. "Barbara!" They say almost in unison.

Jim nods as he recognizes her name. "So I did some checking on you guys, but I could only find books you'd written Mr. Black, on autographs and other collectibles. That made me feel a little safer about contacting you. I flew out to the west coast, but then found out you had checked out of your hotel and was on your way to Paris, which I knew couldn't be a coincidence. I figured I'd ask what you found out and if it was anything fresh, to just go from there."

"But how did you find out we were flying to Paris?" John asks.

"Sorry about that," Stanley says. "Barbara again."

"Yes, the woman at the auction house," Jim says. "She's a real cute girl."

"I know, I know," John says while Stanley smirks.

"You said we were going to hold a press conference anyway John. I figured it was all for public consumption." Stanley says.

"I followed you guys by only a few flights and checked into a hotel a couple of miles from where you ended up and made the call to you after seeing the press conference on the news." Jim says.

"How'd you come across that?" John asks.

"I called your room when I got into town the night before but you weren't answering, so I came by and found out from the bellman that you were holding a press conference. I was going to come by, but thought better of it and waited until the local news aired it. Then I called you again, only this time I got you of course."

"You're a pretty good little detective," John says to him.

Jim shrugs his shoulder. "Not good enough. 40 years and I still don't know who tried to kill me or why."

"Long time to make hypotheses though, right?"

"Sure. I thought it was the government. Like I said, they all had files on us. Maybe they thought we were going to hurt the draft but already a lot were starting to flee into Canada. Nixon, Johnson, I still have no idea who was behind it."

"Well you've outlived them all haven't you?" John says smiling and trying to lift Jim's spirits.

"Oh yeah," Jim says.

"Maybe not," John says, remembering their shadow. "We still aren't sure what's up with our little tail." Shaking off the feeling of insecurity, John realizes he has a golden opportunity in front of him and starts asking major questions. "What do you think about how your music has lasted all these years later?"

Jim, realizing what John's doing, answers, "The crazy part for me is the money. I know my estate makes my family and Pam's and the guys in the group way more than we ever made back then. Money I certainly could have used over the years I might add!"

"Is that who profits?" John asks.

"Yes. Pam got a share but after she died it went to her relatives. My parents, who are now dead, had a share. I guess they willed it somewhere, and the band gets a share of course. I thought my music might last but never expected posters of me to be hanging on young kids' walls this many years later, and movies on the big screen no less!"

"Did you see the Oliver Stone, Val Kilmer film?" Stanley asks.

"Of course, wouldn't you?" John says in a mocking voice.

"Very surreal," Jim answers. "It was a strange experience to see it, and not while being high or drunk at the time either! I felt like the only guy in the world who could set the inaccuracies straight, but Val Kilmer was brilliant. He seemed to be a fan and really tried to channel me to pay homage I think, at least I hope so."

John nods his head. "I've met him, and yes, he is a fan of your work. I'm sure he took it all very seriously. You were never tempted to come forward?" John asks incredulously.

"And what?" Jim asks. "Ask the government to protect me? No never, and my life changed first in degrees and then years upon years added up. There were times eventually, strangely enough, when I felt like I was Richard Phoenix and not Jim Morrison. I just hoped now that you guys had dug up something new and fresh, like you said at your conference.

"I heard all the rumors that I was alive. They say the same thing about Elvis and he sat in an open coffin for God's sake! But you guys said you thought I may have been murdered, and that I had not heard an investigator say before, and after researching your background it appeared you couldn't be a government plant, so I thought I'd take a chance with you.

"I like my life now and really didn't want to uproot it all again, and at my age no less." Shifting in his seat to a more comfortable position, Jim turns the tables on John and Stanley. "So, now it's my turn. What was in the letters that made you start looking at a murder, and what have you found out?"

Stanley interrupts. "May I speak with you for a moment John?"

"Now?" John asks.

"Now," Stanley says firmly.

"Will you excuse us?" John asks Jim as he rises from his chair.

The two walk over to the bar all the while staring back at Morrison. "Convincing story hell, he may be him," Stanley starts, "but what if all of this was a plant to find out what we know? Pick our brains? Worse still, if he's telling us the truth, he knows more than we did!"

"No shit!" John says sarcastically. "Just follow my lead," he says as they walk back to the table.

"Mr. Phoenix, I'm sure you can understand our reluctance to accept if what you're telling us is true at face value."

"Yes. I hadn't thought of that when I came to the west coast and one thing kept me moving to another."

"Yes, I can understand that," Stanley says glaring at John.

"Yes, we all understand each other, but need to be careful. Wouldn't you agree?" John asks.

"Yes of course," Jim replies. "What do you propose? I can't sing for you so don't ask. I'm too old and out of practice."

"No, no," John says.

"Why not? That sounded good," Stanley says. "A private Jim Morrison concert. You are a kill joy John. You could ruin a wet dream!"

"Stop it Stanley. Anyone may be able to impersonate him. I mean, you look like you could be an older Jim Morrison to me I suppose."

"Look," Jim interrupts, "why don't we fly back to Florida to my place I have things kept? There are mementos in a safe deposit box that will prove my story to you. Then if I do that, will you tell me where your investigation has taken you and help me fill in the blanks?"

John and Stanley look at each other and then at Jim. "Yes, but we don't know, or remember, for sure, who is following us and we do know they are in Paris."

"You were followed here?" Jim asks excitedly.

John nods his head yes. "Even our rooms were searched and I don't want to place you at risk after all these years."

"What do you propose then?"

"Let's go to our hotel room first and think this through some more. The boat is about to dock anyway. Maybe we should meet up in Florida. We'll figure something out over some dinner. Sound good?"

"That's fine," Jim replies, "but I wasn't sure about you two either so I got on board first and placed a satchel with some important things in it in a locker on the lower deck in case you were one of the 'black hats' you know? So I need to get it."

"Okay," John says. "Stanley, you go with Jim and I'll meet you on the dock. See that shop over there?" he says pointing to a small shop on the opposite side of the dock. "They have a phone and a net connection. We can check on the hotel and messages before we get there so there are no surprises this time. You guys get Jim's things and meet me there. Sound good?"

"Sounds fine," Jim says.

The boat pulls up to the dock and people start filing off. John leaves the boat and walks across the cobblestone street towards the storefront. His mind is still reeling from the revelations of the last hour. He's really unable to take it all in and wonders what to do. *What would Jim want to do?* This and other questions race through his mind when suddenly, an elderly man in a suit steps swiftly behind him, placing what feels like a gun barrel into his back.

"Hello Mr. Black. How nice to finally meet you," the man says into his ear from behind. "Keep walking, keep walking, straight ahead. You see that barricade to our right? We are going past it then down that alley there to the warehouse behind it."

"The one closed for renovations according to the signs I see?" John asks.

"Exactly."

"And if I don't keep still? What if I scream or run?" John asks, testing the waters.

"I think we both know what will happen if you don't do what I say Mr. Black."

Figuring he has nothing to lose, John questions this mystery man. "Are you the one who won the Morrison letters, or are you the one who killed him?"

The man almost looks disappointed. "You mean I can't be both Mr. Black? How unimaginative. I see you aren't nearly as far along in your little research work than I had given you credit for."

"Well why don't you tell me where I've gone wrong then." John says.

"All in good time Mr. Black, all in good time."

Entering the warehouse makes John's heart sink further. His mind is still reeling but now is trying to figure out whether there is any possibility of escape. At such close range, clearly a sudden movement and he will be shot, but then again, the man with the gun to his back isn't likely to be taking him in the deserted warehouse for a chat and then let him go.

He wonders where Jim and Stanley are and what they would do when he doesn't meet up with them at the little storefront's café. All he can do now is try and talk to the man, reason with him, or try to convince him that he isn't alone and left evidence in the hotel room or elsewhere that others will follow up on in the event that something happens to him.

"You know I'm not here alone," John suddenly says.

"Oh, you mean your assistant and the man you met on the boat? A cop or reporter I believe, or some nut with some information for you? Well, you really should have stayed together when disembarking. 'The buddy system' I think they call it," he says with a soft laugh. "Well, I'm not concerned about them, so don't you be. Okay?"

"You should be. When I don't turn up…"

"They'll what? Call the police and say what?"

Knowing the mystery man is right, John tries to snow him. "You won't get away with harming me," he says more panicked than before.

"Pretty glib talk for a dying man. By the way, who do I have to thank for your curiosity Mr. Black? You couldn't have done all of this by yourself."

"I'm sure I don't know what you mean," John says. "You underestimate me. I figured it all out on my own."

"Oh come now, Mr. Black. You haven't figured anything 'all out' as you put it, even if you do think so."

"What do you mean by that?" John asks.

"The stupid president of the auction house. I suppose he let you read the letters," he says, ignoring John's last remark.

"No, he understood your threats perfectly well." John replies.

"Threats?" he says as he lightly chuckles. "Oh no, he understood my money. It's the American way you know…" He walks around with his gun still aiming at John. "Then if not he, what made you so involved in all of this?"

"You first...you know a lot about me. Whom do I have the pleasure of addressing?" John asks snidely.

"I'm not here to make friends Mr. Black." He raises the gun up to John's eye level. "I'm only going to ask you once more. You've been meddling in things that don't concern you in a very aggressive way since the auction of the Morrison letters in Los Angeles. Why?" he demands to know while shoving the pistol barrel under John's chin.

"Just curious I guess," John says flippantly.

"Well Mr. Black," he says as he removes a silencer from his right jacket pocket and begins screwing it into the pistol, "you know what they say about curiosity and the cat - don't you?"

"Surely if you intend to kill me, you will give me the benefit of knowing who you are and why this is so important to you over 40 years later. You know the statute of limitations has run out on your murder. I couldn't get a cop to care less about you."

"Oh, I'm not concerned about the Morrison affair. Is that what you think? Really Mr. Black, this is so much bigger than you can possibly imagine, or have imagined so far I should say," he says chuckling to himself again. "You can't possibly know or understand what I was doing back then, all those decades ago. How I was helping the next generation and the next... My country... I'm a patriot Mr. Black."

The story begins to sound vaguely familiar so John opts to try running with it. "What's to know Senator?" he asks, taking a stab at Jim's theory.

"Senator? Oh no, you're guessing now. How pathetic. I'm no senator."

"I'm guessing you are or were in some position of power though in the government. A government agency perhaps?"

"You're getting warmer."

"So we have established who you are now," John says.

"Yes, and I know who you are Mr. Black. A world renown expert in authenticating autographs and historical pieces, so why, I had to ask myself, did you come to be meddling in all of this, and I'm not going to ask this question again, in your lifetime at any rate." He lowers the gun sight to John's chest, burying the silencer's tip into it.

"Why grab me now?" John asks. "You obviously ransacked our room in the hotel and you followed us in Los Angeles."

The man shakes his head no. "An associate followed you in Los Angeles, but I admit you forced my trip here to Paris. Me? I'd rather be out golfing but it was the hotel ransacking, as you put it, that we found most interesting."

"We?" John asks.

Ignoring him, the mystery man continues. "I found your notes. How careless to leave them there knowing the room was vulnerable."

John thinks to himself, *He's right on that score.*

"And I saw your appointment with this guy on the boat. Tell me, who does he say he is, and did he give you any information you can use?"

"You're so smart, why don't you figure it out Senator."

"I will. I will because even as we speak, my associate is rounding up your assistant and the man on the boat."

"Look, my assistant is just an employee and is clueless in all of this. How many more people must you kill?"

"Just making an omelet Mr. Black. It was you who drug him into it not me. You hold sole responsibility for what happens to him."

Figuring that reasoning isn't going to work, John resorts to insults. "A madman in a position of power taking the role of God, impulsively snuffing out the lives of innocent people…"

"Innocent people? Mr. Black, I had so wanted to give you more credit in all of this, or at least some understanding, but you really are disappointing me more by the minute. A man who mows down school children with an AK47 is taking the lives of innocent people, but your definition of innocent is a bit broad now isn't it really Mr. Black?"

"Well, in any event, it all backfired on you." John says. "You didn't accomplish your goal of censorship. You didn't stop rock music or the spread of ideas, or the questioning of the government. You failed in every way Senator."

"Did I really?" he asks smiling broadly.

"Yes. You martyred them all. Your plan backfired. Their music, their ideals, all that they stood for, all the more alive in discussion and all the more remembered because of what you did to them."

"I did what had to be done, and you missed the point with your broad, liberal views Mr. Black. Killing them made them heroes perhaps, but to the right people..."

"What do you mean nut case?" John asks, purposely trying to agitate him.

"Nut case? Oh how gauche. You really are reaching now aren't you? By killing them, their kind emulated their dead heroes all the way to the logical conclusion of dying the same way, believing it was hip to do drugs and write meaningless drivel. Dying so misunderstood, tsk, tsk. No, you see, I cleaned up society. I made an effect with these deaths. I didn't fail at all. I did what had to be done."

"You bought those Morrison letters didn't you Senator?"

"Let's just say they will never see the light of day again."

"Well that's okay. I brought the author of them with me today." John says.

"The author? What pitiful trick are you up to now Mr. Black? This is getting old my dear boy and you aren't long for this earth anyway, I'm afraid."

"Senator, it is with great pride that I tell you the man on the boat with me and my assistant was your victim; Jim Morrison."

The mystery man nearly falls over laughing at the comment that just left John's mouth. "This is some stupid joke of yours as a pathetic attempt to save your life. I've heard all the rumors Mr. Black, but you forget I have a more uniquely personal viewpoint on the truth of that urban myth don't you think?

"I mean, you seem to think I killed him, so how could you believe that and that he is alive? I know you're lying now, so if you have nothing else to offer me Mr. Black, I have no choice but to say goodbye to you."

"No, no," John taunts," the joke's on you Senator. Jim Morrison is very much alive."

"Jim Morrison is dead and every school age child knows that Mr. Black. Rumors of fans not withstanding – dead I'm afraid, as you are about to be."

"That may be true, but as far as history tell it man," says the figure stepping out from around the column to face the senator, "but history can be rewritten."

"Jeffrey," the Senator says to his assistant who is holding his arm around Jim's neck, "what have you brought me, and why only one?"

"I couldn't help it. The other one screamed like a little girl and ran off."

"From a gun Jeffrey?"

"We were in a public place boss. I couldn't just start shooting."

"And this one?" he says, gesturing to Jim.

"He came peacefully. Take him from me boss and cover him. I'll call the boys and we'll go find the other one."

"See that you do that Jeffrey. I won't tolerate a screw-up like this again." He looks to Jim. "Move over by your friend here, whoever you are." He waves the gun in John's direction.

"Will you be alright with both of them Mr., I mean Boss?" Jeffrey asks.

"I will be fine. You searched him right?"

"Yes, he has nothing on him. Not even a wallet."

Becoming impatient, the senator orders, "Jeffrey, what are you waiting for? Move out!"

"Right," he says running off.

Turning to look at his newest arrival, he keeps the pistol lowered at John. "Hello. So, you claim to be Jim Morrison. Well you may have fooled Mr. Black here but not me." He looks at John. "Well, tell me Mr. Black, how do you feel that your new friend here is going to because of you?"

"He's a new friend of mine, true enough, but you and he know each other."

"Oh, you mean you really bought his claim to be Jim Morrison?" Turning to Jim, he continues, "You sir, are an imposter and a fool who will die for your folly. Wrong place, wrong time for you my friend, whoever you are."

"No, afraid the joke's on you Senator," John says.

"Stop calling me that! Even if it were true with your Senator remarks, you're a few decades too late. I'm retired now," he says smiling smugly.

"Mr. Morrison, or so you say you are, I have already accomplished what I set out to do. You," he barks while still pointing the pistol at John's head, "I've grown weary of your theatrics Mr. Black, but I will set the record straight for you. All this effort shan't go unrewarded entirely."

"You can do that writing your memoirs from jail Senator, or whoever you are," Jim says.

"Jail? Oh no, that's for common thugs and thieves. I've served my country patriotically, even if no one else had the guts to do so, and history, whoever you are," he says gesturing to Jim, "will remember me for that one day."

Suddenly a third voice is heard in the dimly lit building, sounding near but higher above them all. "No, history will remember you as a pathetic serial killer like the Son of Sam."

"Stanley?" John asks, recognizing his voice.

"Yes John?"

The senator wheels quickly around to see Stanley, but he isn't there. He looks up in the air at a pile of crates just in time to see Stanley duck out of sight behind the top crate.

"You think you can kill us all?" yells Stanley. "Besides, the cops are on their way here John"

"Thank you Stanley!" John shouts in his general direction.

Suddenly, the senator pulls a capsule out of his pocket and holds it near his mouth while backing further away from John and Jim, finally stopping against a row of crates.

"What the hell is that?" John asks.

"Cyanide my dear boy. You think I've given you the answers. Ha! I've merely started you on your journey. The names you've turned up...a mere tip of the iceberg. You'll be discovering all that I've done for my country for years to come.

214

"In the words of another communist who corrupted our people, I believe it was John Lennon who once said, 'whatever gets you through the night' Mr. Black."

"You probably relished his senseless death as well didn't you?" John asks taunting him.

"Relished it? My dear clueless boy, I arranged it!" He aims his gun at John.

"You wouldn't," John says, "you won't. Cowards kill in the darkness. That what you are, a coward, and cowards don't take their own lives."

"That's how you see me in all of this?" the senator asks.

"You know John, you don't always know when to leave well enough alone," Stanley yells.

"Everyone's so big on making a grand entrance these days yet never seem to know how important it is to know when to get off the stage."

"Coward," John repeats.

Nice John, Stanley thinks to himself. *Taunt the man with the cyanide on his lips.*

"You Senator are a coward by any measure of the word!"

"A coward am I?"

"That's my take on it."

"Well then Mr. Black, you really think you have it all figured out don't you? And if you're wrong?"

"Your death will end any more senseless life taking either way."

"Oh John," the senator says, dispensing with formality, "you really get more disappointing the more you speak. Like any good CEO or captain of industry, I have naturally nurtured protégés in many areas and fields who will further my agenda. Will you ferret them out as well my dear boy? Doubtful, extremely doubtful," he says shaking his head. "I see by your face you are shocked to think that there are more following in my work."

"Disgusted maybe, but not shocked," John says.

"But I have said too much already. You are better off going back to the world of make believe Mr. Black. Back to the matrix where everybody else lives so peacefully."

"You killed someone else, not me you moron! An innocent man!" Jim suddenly shouts at the mystery man.

"Oh, we are still playing Jim Morrison are we? Who was your friend that was so innocent then? Jimi Hendrix, Janis Joplin perhaps?"

"You had nothing to do with their deaths," Jim says hopefully.

"Oh didn't I?"

"I meant the innocent young man who killed on my sofa here in Paris all those years ago," Jim says. "I was in the loo that morning when you came in. That boy was just visiting me."

"Spoils of war champ, if what you're saying is true, but I don't take lives. I hire people to do that for me." Shrugging his shoulders he adds, "Good employees are sometimes so hard to find. Perhaps he screwed up."

"Who is the he you mention?" Jim demands.

"Doesn't matter. He had an ugly accident himself soon after." Getting back to the subject at hand, he says, "Look, I don't know if you really are Jim Morrison or just spouting some theory, and more importantly, I don't care. If you are the real deal and came forward now, you'll only be a freak show and no one will understand why you didn't come forward before in all these years."

"Bullshit," John says. "He'll be a hero."

"No, he's right John." Jim says dejectedly.

"And either way, that is why I tied up all my loose ends. Like Pamela Courson…"

"You mother fucker!" Jim says moving suddenly towards the senator.

Just as quickly as Jim moves at him, the senator hits him in the head with the pistol and knocks him to the floor.

John begins to move as the senator speaks, "Uh, stay exactly where you are Mr. Black. I should've already shot you both but I wanted to test my own little theory with that last revelation." He looks to the floor where Jim is still lying. "I'll be damned. You really are Morrison aren't you? How novel… Well Mr. Black," he says while placing the cyanide capsule on the edge of his lips, gently holding it by his teeth, "it looks like your work is just beginning now. You two be good boys and move over to the edge of the wall and turn around or I will swallow this. I'd much rather be about my business before the local cops get here though, but don't worry, we'll meet again I promise."

As John and Jim move towards the wall, still keeping their eyes on him, a giant crash erupts as a wall of crates behind the senator topples over, engulfing him in one fell swoop. Instantly, John grabs at boxes with Jim moving them out of the way, and grabs the pistol when it comes into view lying beside the senator's now motionless body on the blood covered floor.

John stands with the pistol raised over the senator's body. "Do you think he's dead?" he asks Jim. "Stanley!" John yells. "Are you alright? Where are you?"

"Right here chief!" Stanley says, walking up to them. "God I am out of shape. It took much longer than I thought to push those damn things over on him. Thank God they were empty and he didn't move around too much when he was talking to you."

"Where the hell are those cops and what did you tell them?" John asks.

"What cops?" Stanley asks in reply.

"The cops you said you called."

Stanley lightly smiles at his success. "That was for his benefit," he says motioning to the senator on the floor. "My cell phone doesn't work in here."

"Lovely," John says, "then how did you know?"

"After I ran from the guy who jumped Jim and me, I felt pretty bad and doubled back just in time to see the guy walking with Jim into this warehouse. I didn't know what was going on. To be honest, I thought Jim here may have been the bad guy after all, so I crept inside to listen to what was going on and heard you talking to this guy," he says motioning to the man on the floor. "I liked to shit when I realized he had a pistol on you."

"You liked to shit..." John says back to him.

Jim, standing up from having been crouched down over the body says, "He doesn't seem to have a pulse."

"He must have swallowed the pill when he fell." Johns says.

"Maybe not. The pill's on the floor here," he says, bending down and picking up the capsule. "I think he broke his neck actually."

"Now we need to call some cops," John says.

"Okay, but wait," Jim says. "What's going to happen to me now?" He looks at John and Stanley. "I've spent too many years anonymous to show up now."

"Are you kidding? We'll get rich!" Stanley says.

Jim looks at Stanley like he's crazy.

"I mean, you'll get rich," Stanley corrects quickly.

"I never did music to make money Mr. Simpson, only to raise awareness and I lost so many years in fear and hiding, and nobody can give me those back, but I did find myself my friend, and I'd like to leave this world the same man. It's too late for me to change back to the Jim Morrison everyone will expect. Well, you can understand that can't you?"

"Yes of course," Stanley says, still in a state of disbelief.

"Yes, you may count on both of our silence," John says, giving Stanley a dirty look.

"Yeah, yeah," Stanley says, "but think of all that money," he whines.

John looks at Jim and smiles. "You leave. Go on Jim, your secret is safe with us, and we'll get the cops before one of his henchmen report back here. We may have to tell the world that you might have been killed though, which will still rewrite history a bit because we will have to explain why this man tried to kill us, the letters, and all of that."

"I understand but that's okay now. The truth is always okay," Jim says hugging them both. "Thanks again." He slips out the door and throws them the peace sign with his fingers as he goes.

"Wait!" Stanley shouts a moment after the door closes.

"What now Stanley?" John asks.

"Damn, I didn't get his autograph!" Stanley replies.

John shakes his head and with a light smile says, "Oh Stanley…"

About the Author

In the world of collecting there are certain things you always want to keep an eye out for. In the entertainment memorabilia realm, the most important quality an item has is its authenticity. While many dealers can and do sell memorabilia items, not all of them can guarantee that what you're buying is the real thing. Piece of the Past CEO Kevin Martin is one of the few dealers who can.

Having been in the Entertainment and Memorabilia industries for nearly 30 years, Kevin Martin is one of the most sought after signature authenticators in the country. He has published hundreds of articles on the ever-growing field of collecting, as well as having written over a dozen books on everything you'd need to know about collecting celebrity autographs to price guides, and a few others in between. He is a member of the IACC, IADA, Manuscript Society, Ephemera Society, and UACC. Kevin has been called upon to consult with the world's most respected names in the Auction Industry including Christie's and Butterfield's, and has even been tapped for consultation by The Smithsonian Institute.

Piece of the Past, Inc. has spent several years as a major entertainment memorabilia supplier to such companies as Planet Hollywood, Hard Rock Cafe, Field of Dreams, and Disney, among others. Kevin has owned and operated galleries and shops all over the United States. When it comes to experience in a trade dominated by fakes, reprints and forgeries, collectors know that when they want a truly authentic addition to their collections, the first, and usually only, place to call is Piece of the Past.

The 27 Club is his first piece of fictional work with the promise of more to come. His main company, Piece of the Past, is headquartered in Las Vegas, Nevada. He currently resides in Southern California with his wife and two children (with twins on the way!)

For more information about Kevin or Piece of the Past, please visit his website at
www.pieceofthepast.com